# DANCING IN THE RAIN

*A Novella*

www.writingsbyjackie.com

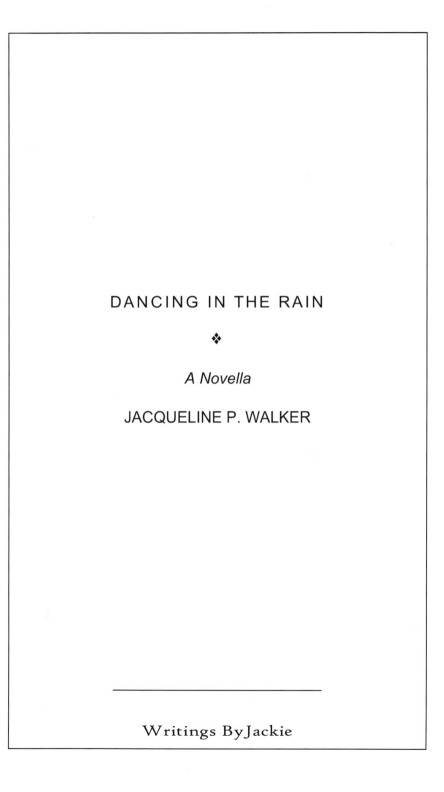

# DANCING IN THE RAIN

❖

*A Novella*

JACQUELINE P. WALKER

---

Writings By Jackie

ISBN: 978-1-7369503-4-0

*Keep watch while you're chasing the sun,*

*for when you least expect it,*

*a storm may be chasing you.*

*—Writings By Jackie—*

# TABLE OF
# CONTENTS

MAY 1997
WASHINGTON, D.C.

# CHAPTER
# ONE

It was an unseasonably hot and gloomy Wednesday afternoon in May 1997. Dark, ominous clouds possessed the sky, and muggy air intensified the stuffiness on the platform in the overcrowded subway station. Maxine Desiree Weldon was sure that a thunderstorm was brewing. But she didn't know that perfect storms of a different kind were barreling toward her—determined to upend her life, career, family, and peace of mind. Instead, that fateful afternoon, thirty-six-year-old "Maxi" was only concerned with beating the rain. The last thing she wanted was to get soaked by a sudden downpour and frightened by thunder and lightning. So, when she exited the subway car and noticed that the escalator wasn't working, she sighed, gritted her teeth, and bounded up the steps, grimacing as the city's foul sounds and smells gushed toward her. Maxi wasn't sure what she hated more, the pushing and shoving in the musty, crowded subway or the heat, humidity, and stench of stale city odors. To add insult to injury, the closer she got to the top of the escalator, the louder the sounds blasted in her earlobes.

*Uh-oh, some kind of commotion or altercation. And right in front of the subway entrance. I don't need to get caught up in this.*

Maxi alighted from the last step of the escalator and gingerly wiggled her way through the crowd, avoiding contact with the bystanders while glancing, curious to see what was going on. She saw two groups that appeared to be middle school kids hurling insults and words (words she wished she didn't have to hear) at each other. One of the boys looked familiar. *Is that Rick? Yep, it is. Somehow, he always finds himself in the middle of an argument or fight.* Maxi had tried her best to keep her son, Gary, from hanging out with him. She paused for a minute to survey the groups. *No, Gary wasn't in the crowd. Thank goodness! Whew. All right, let me walk these blocks quickly. I'm running from the rain like I'm in a movie running from a boulder or a dust cloud.*

It had been a long day. Her boss, Nancy, was on vacation. As Nancy's assigned point of contact, Maxi had been covering a heavy schedule of meetings, responding to executive inquiries, and guiding other staff members while keeping her projects on target. Since Monday, Maxi had been in the mode of early arrival and late departure. Right now, she wanted nothing more than to get home, strip down to her birthday suit, and soak in a hot tub with a shot of lavender aromatherapy oil. *Speaking of shots—a bit of*

*Hennessy might not be a bad idea.* Maxi chuckled but decided to settle for a glass of red wine.

As she continued her walk home from the subway station, Maxi prayed she would not encounter any more neighborhood disturbances. She anticipated the comfort she would feel once she was home. Home and family were Maxi's priorities and where she found joy. She loved her house. It was a brick rowhouse she had bought with her husband, Tony, less than two years ago—a purchase that was an especially significant accomplishment. It took sacrifice and every bit of their savings but being a homeowner and having that home in a historic Washington, D.C. neighborhood made Maxi beam proudly. Now, her house wasn't one of the shining stars on the block, but Maxi knew it was an investment—a foundation to build a legacy for generations. The three-story rowhouse, built during the early 1900s, had 1200 square feet of living space: three bedrooms, one bathroom, a separate living room, and a dining room, along with a small galley kitchen (in need of complete renovation and new appliances). There was also a partially finished basement, which Maxi's husband had claimed as his space. The small front porch was one of the best-selling points; Maxi enjoyed sitting outside and catching the activities of the neighborhood.

The gated back driveway allowed for off-street parking for one vehicle, which was another plus to help avoid break-ins or tampering, which were often frequent in city living. Admittedly, the house could stand a little love and care, but Maxi and Tony were taking it slow: their one significant investment to date was adding a bathroom, as Maxi was unwilling to share her bathroom with guests. She barely wanted to share it with her husband. Soaking in the tub was her escape, her time to lock out evil thoughts, stressful experiences, and sorrowful circumstances. It was her time to daydream—to visualize her heart's desires—and immerse herself in the vision of making them real.

Maxi loved living in the city. Washington, D.C., was home, although she had never forgotten her native land. The eldest of three children, she was born in Jamaica; she moved to the D.C. area as a teenager to join her mother, Leonie, who had previously migrated there seeking a better life for her family. Until she was eight years old, Maxi's life in Jamaica was void of turmoil. She lived with her parents and two younger siblings in a small house in an upcoming neighborhood. Maxi held treasured memories of those years. She recalled walking to school, playing with neighborhood friends, walking with her siblings to church on Sundays, occasionally visiting with extended family, and sharing memorable family outings and conversations.

Then things changed. Her father left Jamaica when Maxi was eight years old. That was the last time she laid eyes on him. It was supposed to be a short visit with his brother in Harlem, NY, a survey visit to determine if he could make a life there for the family. But he never sent for Leonie, Maxi, and her brothers and never returned home. They weren't very concerned during his first few months away. He sent letters and money and even managed to call a few times. But as the months turned into years, notes, money, and calls dwindled until they disappeared. He'd found something or someone more appealing in Harlem, and just like that, he let his family go.

Barely thirty years old when her husband left, Leonie Weldon had been married for ten years. The eldest of six children, Leonie was a quiet girl who learned to work hard at a young age, helping her parents on their farm: planting, watering, reaping, and caring for the chickens. She blossomed as a teenager, growing curvy with smooth, mocha-colored skin, piercing eyes fashioned with sparkling onyx pupils, and a neatly formed three-inch Afro displayed on a five-foot seven-inch frame. It certainly wasn't surprising that Leonie attracted attention whether she wanted to or not.

Leonie had met her husband at nineteen. She was still living at home, helping with the farm, and working part-time at the local store in town. Back then, she didn't have big dreams; she had grown accustomed to life's routine. Then, one day, hearing, "hello," she looked up, and there stood a young man at least six inches taller than she was, with pecan-colored skin, shoulders broad and solid, muscles everywhere, and the biggest grin revealing a God-given perfect set of pearly white teeth. He was delivering milk to the store—a new job for him. From that day on, life was never the same for Leonie. Her newfound friend shared stories of the city, music, and dancing—exciting stories she could hardly imagine. Leonie was smitten, and her curiosity about life away from the farm consumed her thoughts.

Leonie's father was less than enamored with the young man and the idea that his daughter was in a relationship. She was a little girl in his eyes, and he expected her to remain that way forever. But Leonie was in love and yearned to see new places and experience new things. So, less than a year after meeting, the two lovebirds ran off to get married and start a new life in the city. Two years into the marriage, Leonie gave birth to Maxi.

Ten years later, her husband had run off again—but without her. Now a single parent, Leonie did her best to make ends meet. She worked odd jobs cooking and cleaning from Monday to Thursday. On Fridays and Saturdays, she worked eight to ten hours at Prosperity—the most frequented dry cleaner in the city. It was hard work running the cash register, servicing customers, handling dangerously hot equipment, and carefully assembling clothes for pickup. And then, if that wasn't enough, she had to sort through the growing mountain of jumbled, intertwined wire hangers thrown in the empty room adjoining the cashier area because, in those days, customers didn't get to take the hangers with them. It was a cost-saving move, but it made for an annoying task of sorting and stringing the hangers for reuse. There was no joy in Leonie's work. It was what she had to do to feed, clothe, and shelter her children. She never spoke to Maxi or the kids about their father's sudden disappearance, and they never questioned her about it. In fact, Maxi realized that only about three years ago (more than twenty-five years after her father had moved to Harlem), Leonie took her daughter's advice to work with an attorney to ensure she was *officially* divorced.

Four years after Maxi's father vanished from their lives, Leonie continued to struggle, and things seemed to get more challenging by the day. Maxi was in fifth grade and preparing to take the Common Entrance Examinations—a national test to secure a place in the country's high school system, covering what is akin to seventh through twelfth grades in the USA. At that time, Leonie received an unexpected opportunity to visit the USA (Washington, D.C.) and maybe find a way to stay and bring her children. After much soul-searching, Leonie sent Maxi and her brothers to stay with Maxi's aunt, who lived two neighborhoods away and then hopped on a flight to D.C.

If Leonie had thought life and work were hard in Jamaica, she didn't find much relief in the USA. She had domestic jobs, not merely laundry and cooking but washing, waxing, and polishing floors on her knees. She collected and hauled trash from offices and cleaned public bathrooms filled with bacteria and a stench more powerful than the odors of bleach or disinfectant. Yet Leonie soldiered on, knowing her goal was to ensure that her kids would never have to do the things she had to do to live. She wanted a better life for her children. She didn't want them merely to dream; she wanted them to make those dreams real. Finally, about four years after moving to D.C., Leonie secured passage for Maxi and her brothers to join her there.

Just before her sixteenth birthday, Maxi arrived in Washington, D.C., and Leonie enrolled her in the local high school, where they placed her in the tenth grade. Before starting school, she had heard that many of her fellow immigrants had difficulty fitting in merely because they spoke differently (patois dialect) or weren't in tune with the latest and greatest styles or slang. And she saw it happen all around her—the conflicts, the slurs about the *nasty food she ate,* or the *huts* she lived in back in Jamaica. She

9

never really knew where she mustered the strength not to allow the words to defeat her, but somehow, she managed to hold on to her confidence and self-esteem. Maxi adjusted quickly to her new environment and culture. Her big smile, easy-going personality (like the way she brushed aside ignorant insults and deflected conflict), as well as obvious academic smarts (like her track record of getting good grades and offering help on assignments) quickly won the attention and approval of key classmates, especially Devin Delaney, the star high school basketball player. Devin's validation helped to pave the way for her acceptance on a larger scale. Soon enough, she had a close circle of friends.

Immediately, Maxi was taken in by Devin's good looks. He was *hot*. He stood at six feet three inches and 185 pounds with not an ounce of fat—all lean muscle. His light tan complexion was what Black people called "redbone." Those enticing gray-blue eyes sparkled like a beautiful pair of topaz, and his brown, curly hair hung down without help from using a Jheri curl kit that became popular during the eighties. Devin was always confident and self-assured. Maxi liked Devin's looks but knew he was also attracted to what she had to offer. Her mother had always told her she was pretty as a picture. Maxi's complexion was somewhere between her mother's mocha and her father's pecan skin colors. But she definitely had her mother's riveting jet-black eyes. Her thick, curly hair that hung to her shoulders and a small helping of her mother's hypnotizing curves made it no surprise that she turned heads and captured the interest of the most popular student in her class.

Devin and Maxi became inseparable. They were young

and in love. Maxi had many hopes for their future together, but they never fully blossomed. *Trifling somebody he turned out to be!* Maxi shook her head as she remembered being seventeen and pregnant. Then she teared up, recalling that she had not carried that pregnancy to term. From time to time, she wondered if that baby would have been a boy or a girl and what would he or she have become. It's been nineteen years, but the memory lingered. Especially on days like today when dark clouds lingered, the atmosphere jarred her memory and triggered a mode of reflection of those times.

As she thought about it, Maxi remembered that at the time, the most surprising thing to many was that they (Maxi and Devin) didn't end their relationship—instead, they grew even closer. She recalled his promise, "Oh, I got you, baby. We're gonna be together forever, and I'm gonna take care of you," she muttered out loud, mocking his words as she continued her trek home. *It's a good thing I did, as my momma told me: I went to college part-time and worked while he went to college and played basketball.*

Devin played for four and a half years in the National Basketball Association (NBA). It was during that time, some seven years after her miscarriage, that Gary was born. Maxi and Devin were excited and happy. But their happiness was short-lived. Devin's NBA career ended a year and a half later, and he was forced to play overseas. He wasn't happy that he hadn't soared in the NBA as he had expected, and he didn't enjoy going from country to country, year after year, to make a decent living. But Devin couldn't figure out a solid, permanent alternative and never had a fallback plan. For him, it was basketball or nothing. He also

11

couldn't get rid of the flunkeys or parasites that pretended to be his friends. Devin always basked in the glory of being the popular guy. He surrounded himself with friends who were at his beck and call, friends who literally worshipped him but always expected a favor in return. Some of these friends or followers were known to dip and dabble in things and events that challenged Maxi's values and the law. But Devin was never concerned. "My hands are clean," he would always say to Maxi. "Just because I hang with them doesn't mean I do *everything* they do." Maxi's problem was deciphering what Devin would or wouldn't do. He never said, "I don't do *anything* they do." Instead, he said, I don't do *everything* they do." *There's a big difference between not doing anything and not doing everything.*

Also, one of the things that seemed to come with Devin's basketball career was a disturbing Jekyll-and-Hyde personality. He got increasingly outspoken and even unkind to his friends. He became Dictator Devin—expecting to be first at everything, instigating arguments, challenging every opinion, and reveling in the attention. Maxi witnessed instances of Devin initiating and escalating fights among his cronies. He mastered dropping words to intensify the argument, then grinning as he fueled the fire and watched them go at it. Those scenes were the beginning of the end of Maxi's dedication to Devin. She didn't like inciting fights and didn't want to be a party to it.

Slowly it seemed a wall appeared between them. At home with Maxi, Devin grew quieter, seeming to internalize thoughts and concerns that she couldn't get him to express. He became angry more and more if she questioned his mood. He ridiculed her career dreams, referring to them as "petty or insignificant." *I showed up for all his bas-ketball games, but he couldn't show up for my college gradua-tion ceremony. "It's only night school," he said. "What's the big deal?"*

During the early years, Devin doted on their son, Gary. He took him just about everywhere he went. "My little man," Devin called him. But as he spent more time with his crew and drifted into moodiness, he also paid less and less attention to Gary. He was even impatient with the child's natural curiosity and desire to go out with his father regu-larly, as the boy had gotten used to doing.

Although her devotion was waning, Maxi still loved Devin during those years. She immersed herself in thoughts of the past and how he made her feel when his crew wasn't as dominant in his life. She longed to return to the time when she could talk to him about her dreams, and he would listen intently without interruption, encouraging her and comforting her. Maxi hung on to the memory of how Devin gave her a sense of belonging in high school, easing her transition between cultures. She was grateful to him, so she hung on. But after a few years of ups and downs, Devin began spending more time with his street crew and had multiple stints of four or more months playing over-seas. And as their time together and contact lessened, the relationship crumbled.

*Then, that fool deserted us. He went away to play overseas. Brazil, I think it was, and never came back. Lucky for me, we weren't married, which made moving on much more effort-less. And now it's been six years since Gary has seen his fa-ther—well, maybe not six, since we ran into him in the grocery store once. Trifling! And he certainly doesn't seem to know the meaning of child support. Did I say trifling already? I never filed for child support. I know I should go after him for the money, but right now, I feel it's better to leave him wherever he's at—avoid the complications. Besides, Tony is a great father figure for Gary.*

Gary was Maxi's pride and joy. Already five-feet seven-inches and only twelve years old, Maxi predicted he would eventually tower over her. Slender, with long limbs like his father, Gary also inherited those sparkling gray-blue eyes and had a head full of curls—except they were black, the color of Maxi's hair. Lately, the two had been having a friendly war about his hair. Gary wanted to wear his hair in cornrows as he saw them getting increasingly popular with celebrities and athletes. But Maxi wasn't quite ready for that. She was uncomfortable with the reaction and unfavorable attitudes that her son might have to deal with outside their culture and community. Plus, she wasn't going to braid his hair constantly, and paying for the upkeep was not an expense she wanted to add to her budget.

Like his father, or maybe because of his father, he was addicted to basketball. Maxi had to admit he was a pretty good player and got better daily. She didn't mind his athletic focus as long he balanced it with academics.

"Whew," Maxi sighed; she had covered the first two blocks. She had only about a block and a half left, but today's walk seemed like the longest mile. She was tired and hoped her husband, Tony, the jokester, wasn't home thinking up some new foolish prank to trap her. *Like that Saturday morning when I was home alone and suddenly heard that*

*creepy whistling sound. It freaked me out, and I couldn't fig-ure out where it was coming from. It would stop and start. Of course, I thought the house was haunted, and we had to find a way to give it back! Finally, I couldn't take it and sat outside on the porch waiting for him to return from the hardware store. Then I discovered that, because he knows I'm a scaredy cat, he had wired some noisy contraption on a timer in the basement for a laugh. It wasn't funny— well, maybe a little.*

Truth be told, Maxi loved Tony's sense of humor as much as she loved the piercing stare of his jet-black eyes (much like her own) and the comforting embrace of his toned body. Although she hated admitting it, his towering six-foot, five-inch frame, and 225-pound muscular body reminded her of her father. But his lightheartedness, hu-mor, finding ways to make her smile, and diligence as a provider and father were the traits that truly warmed her heart, and she prayed they would never fade away. Still, as much as she loved his pursuit of joy and laughter, today was not a day for jokes. *There is a time, and today isn't the day. I'm tired.*

Born and raised in Washington, D.C., twenty-eight-year-old Tony Vernay had seen his share of drama and tragedy. On his twelfth birthday, he helplessly watched as a dispute over a card game escalated, resulting in his father lying dead in the street from a gunshot wound. That trag-edy significantly impacted Tony for many years. With-drawn, he played hooky from school so often that his ab-sences rose well beyond the official truancy level. Finally, he quit. But he successfully passed the General Education Development (GED) test and enlisted in the army, serving seven years before earning an honorable discharge. After being introduced by a mutual friend, Tony and Maxi married almost three years ago.

*Things have not been easy for Tony. I guess that's why he plays so much—that's his therapy. We all have something! He's still my baby, though. I tell him that all the time. And with his sweet baby face, people constantly question his age and whether he is more like twenty-one than twenty-eight. But he is twenty-eight; I've seen the birth certificate.* Maxi chuckled. *But back to reality, I'm not in the mood for jokes or pranks today.*

It had been a hectic week at work. Wednesday—hump day—lived up to its name. Overwhelmed by a schedule of seemingly endless meetings, Maxi had barely gotten any real work done all week. She had to figure out how to catch up on Thursday and Friday. She was stressed, and trying to hurry home and beat the storm only intensified that feeling and made her nervous and almost anxious.

*Boom!* Out of nowhere came a rumble of thunder. Maxi ran as fast as she could, somehow making it up the steps to her home, where she dropped her bags and plopped into the porch chair to catch her breath. Except for getting hit by a few drops of rain, she had missed the storm by a hair. Still, instead of going inside, Maxi remained seated on the porch. Something about the rain captured her attention—the water blowing in the wind (some drops had made their way to where she was sitting) felt refreshing. The sweet scent of the wet earth overtook the unpleasant smell of the humid air and smoky vapor rising from the concrete. Maxi took it all in for a few minutes. It reminded her of her original home—Jamaica—and her childhood. She smiled as she recalled playing in the rain as a child and how much she had enjoyed it—unlike now when she had no desire to get rain-soaked. But she still savored the smell of nature and the wet earth. It was refreshing and somehow calming.

*Boom*! Another thunderous bolt and flash of lightning brought Maxi back from her daydream. She had better get inside. As she stood up, it dawned on her that while she had been reflecting, she hadn't heard a sound or seen a figure move about inside the house. The shutters on the front windows were closed, which typically only happened at night or when everyone was away. It wouldn't surprise her if Tony weren't home, but where was Gary? He should have been home by now. She hoped he hadn't got caught in the storm. *I'd better get inside and see what's going on.*

Maxi turned on the light in the hallway as she entered the foyer. Although nightfall was several hours away, with the shutters closed and the stormy skies, it was a little dark. She heard a voice coming from the kitchen: Gary's. As she approached, she could hear him better; clearly, he was on the phone.

"Yeah, I didn't stay 'cause nobody was hanging around. It looked like rain," he spoke into the receiver.

Maxi waved, blew a kiss, and softly whispered, "Hey, baby. Glad you weren't out there in the storm."

"Hi, Mom, yeah," he responded, seemingly surprised to see her. "I…I gotta go. Mom's here," he continued nervously.

Maxi couldn't hear the response from the caller well enough to recognize the voice. But she noticed Gary tapping on the counter and looking up at the ceiling. Then he interjected a sentence or two and suddenly cut off the caller.

"All right, all right, I'll, I'll see…tomorrow. Yeah, yeah, I mean it. Tomorrow. Okay, bye." He hung up the receiver, walked over, and hugged and kissed Maxi. "Hey, Mom, you're dry, so you didn't get caught in the storm either," he said, turning away quickly.

When Maxi hugged him, she felt a tension in his body and caught a hint of nervous stuttering in every word he said. It seemed odd to her.

"I caught a stroke of luck and just missed getting soaked. Did you have a good day? Everything all right?" Maxi responded, noticing that he had now walked to the kitchen sink, where she couldn't see his face or expression.

Gary turned, gave her a quick look, and turned back, twisting the faucet and busily washing the few items in the sink, "Yeah. Huh, that was just Rick. You know, Rick, who lives two blocks over. He was wondering where I was after school. I didn't hang around at the basketball court today—no need. I could tell it would rain."

*Hmm, Rick? The same guy that I just saw at the subway getting into it with a bunch of other kids.*

"Well, that was a good decision. No point putting yourself in harm's way."

"Yeah," answered Gary, chuckling nervously.

Maxi was suspicious. Something was afoot, but she was wise enough to know when to press, lecture, delay a response, or let it go. She changed the conversation—for now.

"Tony's not home, is he?" Maxi asked, changing the subject to ease her discomfort.

"Ah, no, Mom. I forgot. He called. He'll be a couple of hours late. He said we don't have to wait on him for dinner.

But he'll be here as quickly as possible—at least by the time you have your nightly dessert."

Surprised, Maxi rolled her eyes and asked, "'Nightly dessert?' What's that supposed to mean?"

Gary looked around from the sink, shrugged his shoulders, and answered sarcastically, "Mom, I'm just delivering the message. You always tell me to be specific when someone gives me information to share with you."

"Seriously, Gary? You know you're a smart aleck, but I'll let it go. I'll be upstairs. I need to relax—bath time. Then, I'll fix dinner."

Gary nonchalantly shrugged his shoulders. "All right."

Maxi exited the kitchen and started up the stairs.

*Nightly dessert! It appears my husband believes that I am a sweet freak. Well, I am. But I will not admit it to him or Gary. For some reason, it seems from Gary's attitude that something is bothering him. But I'm tired, so I'm not going to think about it right now.*

JACQUELINE P. WALKER

CHAPTER
# TWO

Maxi and Gary sat quietly at dinner. Except for saying grace and amen, they didn't say too much. When Tony was there, laughter and conversation were almost nonstop. Tony couldn't help sharing some incredulous and hilarious stories he had heard. But even when he wasn't there, Maxi and Gary typically had great conversations. Sometimes it was about something they had heard or experienced that day, something on TV, or something Gary wanted or wanted to do. Today was different. Maxi was tired from the long hours she'd put in the last week covering for her boss, and the dreary weather wasn't helping.

*Maybe that's it. The weather has gotten to us both: heat, humidity, dark skies, thunder, and pouring rain—mood busters.*

*Thud, thud, thud, thud, thud! Slam!* Maxi knew that was Tony coming up the backstairs from the driveway.

"Hey, hey! Is everybody well? The rain cooled things

down a bit," he rambled, excitedly removing his shoes as he stepped inside the back foyer. Then he swung open the door that led to the kitchen and adjoining dining area.

Maxi smiled. *Tony always makes an entrance (unless he's sneaking up on you with some prank). Otherwise, he's as loud as anyone can get. You never have to wonder if he's arrived—he'll announce himself.*

"Hey, babe, you had a good day despite the rain and long hours?" Tony asked, smiling. He walked over and kissed her cheek loudly while hugging her around the shoulders and playfully shaking her from side to side.

"Hey, babe, it was all right. Busy is my only complaint. Glad you're home. How was your day?" Maxi answered, perking up.

"Hey, Tony," Gary mumbled.

"Hey, young man, what's up? I got the Knicks tonight. Who are you feeling?" asked Tony, pounding his chest with a big grin.

"Man, you're tripping. I'm sticking with the Heat," Gary responded with a quick, short smile while motioning a chest pound.

"All right, all right, we'll see."

"I'm not even worried about it. It's all good," Gary said.

"Okay, okay. I like your confidence," Tony said, offering a high five, which Gary returned.

"Why did you both look so sad when I walked into the room? I didn't hear a sound coming up the stairs. And when I came in, you were sitting here playing with your food instead of eating. You all missed me? Is that it?" he asked, placing the shopping bag on the counter. "I'ma wash up quickly and come eat with you all. Maybe my presence will liven things up a bit."

"All right, Mr. Life of the Party, I'll make your plate."

As Maxi stood up, Tony held her chin and landed a quick, sweet kiss on her lips. Maxi smiled.

"Oh, let me put this in the refrigerator," Tony said teasingly, lifting the shopping bag from the counter. "I'll be back in a few."

Just that brief exchange with Tony lifted Maxi's spirit. Turning to Gary, she grinned and said, "He's in rare form tonight, uh? What's he got in that bag? Should I peek?"

"That's on you," was Gary's curt response.

"You're no fun! But I'll leave his little shopping bag alone," Maxi answered, sticking her tongue out at Gary and proceeding to fix Tony's plate.

Gary shook his head and continued picking at his dinner.

Maxi glanced at Gary with slight concern. *Maybe he's just tired. I'm tired today. It's not like he's been exceptionally quiet or moody for weeks or days, so I won't say anything, but I'll keep an eye on him.*

As soon as Tony sat at the table, his gung-ho, upbeat mood made a difference. Gary and Maxi perked up, engaging in conversation.

"Hey, son, you think the Heat are about to beat the Knicks again?"

"No doubt. The Knicks can't come close to the Heat. And anyone who thinks they can doesn't know anything about *basketball!*" Gary replied enthusiastically.

"Uh-oh, that's a serious statement, young man, almost threatening to a dude like me who grew up playing street ball," Tony answered, laughing loudly, clearly tickled at

23

Gary's comment.

"I'm just saying, it is what it is," Gary replied.

"And where do you stand?" Tony asked, turning to Maxi.

"I'm for real with Gary; the old Knicks can't beat the Heat," she said slowly and deliberately. "But it doesn't matter because whoever wins can't get past the Bulls and Jordan anyway. So, choose your loser!"

"Yeah, Mom, that's what I'm talking about," Gary chimed in.

"Ouch, mother and son ganging up on me. I'm outnumbered," Tony said, holding his chest and motioning in shock.

"Well, I'll give you all the second half of that about the Bulls, but I'm holding out for the Knicks."

"Hold on tightly, old man; you might hit some speed bumps," Gary replied, laughing hysterically. Maxi joined him.

"Okay, I'll save the rest of this talk until later during the game. Miz lady hasn't had her tea and crumpets for the evening. Let me put the kettle on and get that hot water boiling to make her tea nice and hot the way she likes it."

"Crumpets? "Okay, now you're being funny," said Maxi.

"You know, I mean your dessert. You're the one who told me you drink tea with your dessert because it's the British cultural influence that you picked up in Jamaica. I'm just supporting you, Max" he responded.

"You know you were being cute with the crumpets thing instead of just saying dessert. What do we have anyway?" asked Maxi.

"Oh, no worries, I brought you something special: a

cake," Tony said, retrieving the shopping bag from the refrigerator and pulling out a box he placed in front of Maxi.

Excited at the thought of a cake, Maxi quickly opened the box. She laughed out loud as she closed the box.

"What is it?" asked Gary curiously.

"What's the matter? Don't you like the cake? I had it made just for you!" Tony declared with a big grin.

Maxi pursed her lips, shook her head, and stared at Tony as she again opened the box and pushed it towards Gary. "It's a FISH cake. He brought home a fish cake."

"Oh, snap, it is! Look at the eyes," said Gary with surprise.

"That's it. That's it right there. It's cake, but it's like an ESCOVITCH FISH with the head on and the eyes, just like you enjoy, so what's the problem?" Tony asked excitedly. "It looks good, and I bet it tastes good. The lady that made this can bake, and she's from the islands too. And it's that black rum cake. That's the cake under the fisheyes and all," he proudly explained.

"Is it really?" asked Maxi. "You know that's my weakness. That and the escovitch fish, so you figured you'd get two for one?" She chuckled.

"Come on now. I hooked you up. Here, taste it." He placed a small plate and a knife on the table in front of Maxi.

Picking up the knife, Maxi snickered and commented, "Okay, I think I'll cut the tail first. I'm not sure I'm ready for the head and those bulging eyes." She cut a small piece of the cake and bit into it apprehensively. "Oh, wow, it's delicious!".

"See, I knew I did good!" Tony countered happily.

"You did," replied Maxi, "although we know you thought it was funny. But I'll even go for those eyes; this cake tastes so good. Thank you, honey." She puckered her lips, and Tony proudly planted a kiss on them.

"You guys want to try it?" Maxi asked.

"Naw, I'll get the dishes and then go down and get ready to put some *heat* on somebody!" Gary replied.

"Did you hear that? He got jokes. Baby, let me get your tea. Save me some cake for tomorrow. I need to keep my sugar rush low for the evening, this way I can calmly share my basketball knowledge with the youth," he answered. "Enjoy your tea and crumpets and feel free to join us if you want to watch the game," Tony said.

"No, thanks. I'll have my treat and then read a bit. I'll probably turn in a little early. I need to get to the office as early as possible to get caught up. Today was overrun with meetings. I couldn't get any real work done." Maxi sighed.

"Okay, baby, I'll snuggle up with you later. Right now, I'm about to school this young man on picking the winning team!" Tony said excitedly, hopping down the basement stairs.

Maxi closed her eyes as she savored her last bite.

*Smooch!* Maxi planted a loud kiss on Tony's cheek, waking him up.

"You're leaving already?" he groaned, noticing she was fully dressed.

"Yes, dear. I told you I had to get in early this morning. You need to get up soon and ensure Gary gets up and out on time."

"Yes, ma'am. Anything else, ma'am?"

"That's it for now. I'm gone. Love you."

"Love you, babe," Tony said between yawning and sitting up in bed.

"Love you too," Maxi said, blowing a kiss from the doorway before heading downstairs. She didn't bother to stop by Gary's room. She had a full schedule and wanted to stay on target.

"Hey, Gary, you up?" Hearing no response, Tony walked over and pounded his fist on the door twice.

"Yeah, I'm getting up. I'm getting up," Gary answered, whining.

"All right, you know your momma will kill me if I don't get you up and make sure you get out of here on time for school," replied Tony.

"I know. I'm about to shower," Gary responded.

"Good, we can leave together. I'll drop you at the subway," Tony replied.

"Oh, okay," Gary said quietly.

Tony was in the kitchen devouring a bowl of cereal when Gary finally made his way down.

"Hey, Tony, you can leave without me. I'm going to sit here and reread these last chapters. I read them yesterday, but I better refresh before the first period, and I don't like reading on the subway—I might not even get a seat," Gary rambled as he pulled a book from his bag and sat at the table.

"You sure? Aren't you even going to grab some cereal, though? Breakfast is important, and I promised your momma you'd be on time. Don't make a liar out of me," Tony responded, raising his eyebrows.

"I'm not. I'll get cereal, a banana, and juice before going. I've been the last one out before. I'm not going to be late, and I'm not going to miss school. I promise," Gary answered, pleading.

"All right, all right. Let me wash this bowl and get out of here. I'll lock the back door, now all you have to do is lock the front door," Tony replied.

"Thanks, Tony! I've got it."

"Okay, son, have a good day. Remember what I always say?"

"Focus! I will focus. Have a good day," Gary responded, holding his hand up for a high five.

Tony accepted the high-five and added a hug before exiting.

Gary read for a few minutes, then grabbed the telephone and dialed.

"Hey, boy, what's up? Are you ready?" came the voice at the other end before he could even say hello.

"Yes, sir, I'll meet you at the end of the block in ten minutes," Gary answered.

He kept his word. Within ten minutes, he was standing at the end of the block, looking around nervously. Then he sighed a breath of relief as a green sedan pulled up. Gary jumped in on the front passenger side, and the car sped off.

# CHAPTER
# THREE

Maxi's office was adjacent to a subway station with an exit leading to an underground court- yard that allowed entrance to the building with- out going outside. The large structure stood ten floors high with a mirrorlike façade, presenting an opulent appear- ance that it did not live up to on entry. Most individual of- fices were tiny and boxlike, without windows to the exte- rior. In the middle of each floor was an array of cubicles, locked together in groups of four. Also, someone had the bright idea to make the cubicle walls reach only eye level so that the occupants could talk to each other without a barrier—in other words, without a privacy wall. Maxi was fortunate that her boss had gone to bat for her, and, as a re- sult, she was one of the few non-managers assigned an in- dividual office.

"Good morning, Maxi!"

Shocked by the greeting, Maxi turned around. She

wasn't expecting anyone else to be in the office this early. Having exited the elevator still deep in thought, trying to decide which task to tackle first, Maxi hadn't noticed the light creeping out from the slightly open office door. It was Thursday, and Nancy wasn't returning from vacation until Monday. But that was undoubtedly her office and, indeed, her voice.

Nancy Mattison, a demanding perfectionist, was Maxi's director. Over the years, the two developed a good rapport and an effective working relationship. Although they didn't always agree on the methods for getting things done, each admired the other's ability to achieve quality results quickly. Nancy was thankful to have Maxi on her staff for several reasons. First, Maxi was bright, personable, hard-working, and results oriented. Then, Maxi was always there to smooth things over when Nancy upset other departments with her "do it my way and in my time" attitude.

Maxi walked back, stuck her head in the door opening, and, with a look of bewilderment, babbled, "Good morning to you, Nancy! And welcome back. What a surprise! First, I wasn't expecting you back today. Second, you're early. Did you get up with the rooster or something? You're a regular ten o'clock arrival. It's not even seven-thirty. Is this a new thing—like an after-vacation resolution or something?"

Nancy looked up from her computer, pulled off her glasses, sighed, clenched her teeth, and then chuckled. "No such thing, my dear. My husband was called back to the office for an emergency, and as a result, we flew in last night. I thought about staying home alone. Then I figured, why waste two days of leave? So here I am. But as for this early arrival, it's one and done. Don't expect me to be here every day at the crack of dawn!"

"All right, I got you. At least, I hope you enjoyed the days you were gone."

"I did. I did. I'll tell you all about it later."

Taking a hint, Maxi continued, "Well, I'm trying to get a head start myself, so let me get to my desk. I know you may need clarification and updates, so reach out. I'm here."

"Thanks, Maxi. I'll be reaching out to everyone for an update—especially you."

Still, a bit taken aback by Nancy's sudden appearance, Maxi opened the door to her office. *Let me get to work; I can probably get caught up on my stuff now that Nancy is back to do hers, although coming back from vacation on Thursday is different. But, whatever.*

It was already mid-May. With only a month and a half before mid-year reporting, Maxi wanted to ensure her twenty client portfolios remained on target to meet financial expectations. Any adverse reporting could result in losing an account, which would not benefit her or the company. Before you know it, June 30th would be upon her. Maxi had devised a plan to do a deep-dive review of each portfolio by the beginning of June to allow herself a minimum of thirty days if anything appeared out of sorts. The marketing department had also scheduled a meeting to discuss new trend reporting needs. At least for the moment, Maxi shrugged off Nancy's early arrival and strange return on a Thursday and got to work.

As Maxi waded through her emails, the first word in the title of one entry jumped out at her: DEFAULT. *Default, what in the world? How does an account with over three million dollars on hand default on a three-hundred-and-fifty-thousand-dollar payment? Let me take a quick look at recent transactions and reports.*

Unable to find a clue in anything she reviewed, Maxi called her contact at the bank. The two quickly realized that a data entry error had caused the default. The bank had incorrectly updated the account files. Somehow, someone had inadvertently omitted a zero. Instead of displaying $3,000,000, it showed $300,000. As such, when the $350,000 payment request came in, it defaulted.

On hearing the explanation, Maxi rolled her eyes in disbelief. Then, calmly but firmly speaking to her bank contact, she issued directions that she had already crafted in her mind "Maxi style."

"Okay, here's the game plan. You must escalate a data fix, rectify this payment immediately, and any other that has been presented. Get something in place to hold incoming requests (before the fix) instead of automatically defaulting on them. And I need the data corrected before the end of the business day! I will get into "PR" mode and communicate with my client and payees. Plus, I will certainly share the issue, plan, and status with my management, as you should do with yours. Please keep me updated on the progress and thank you for making this a priority. Bye now." Maxi hung up the phone.

No sooner had Maxi turned her focus back to the work she needed to complete than there was a knock on her slightly open office door, and a figure appeared, nervously whispering, "Hey, Maxi, do you have a minute?"

"Oh, yes, come on in, Melissa. What's the matter?" Maxi asked curiously.

Melissa, like Maxi, was a financial analyst on Nancy's staff. Melissa had worked for the company for ten years. She had started as an administrative assistant and worked her way up the ladder while taking evening and weekend classes to earn an accounting degree. When the firm hired Nancy to head the department a little over two years ago, the original staff left abruptly—some say involuntarily. Nancy then hired Melissa (internally) and Maxi (externally) as financial analysts and filled the other roles to round out the department's staff.

Closing the door behind her, Melissa approached Maxi's desk and continued whispering uneasily, "Have you heard?"

"Heard what?" asked Maxi, getting concerned. Although she worked well with Melissa, their conversation was typically about business. But now it seemed Melissa was approaching her about something confidential.

"The layoffs. They're having layoffs," Melissa revealed, seemingly relieved to have gotten the sentence out.

"Who's having layoffs?" asked Maxi, both concerned and confused.

"We are. The company is having layoffs. This week," continued Melissa.

"What? Where did you hear that?" Maxi demanded.

"I can't tell you that. But I believe it," Melissa answered. "Come on, Maxi; I bet it's today. Nancy is back from vacation on Thursday! Doesn't that seem weird?"

"Yes, I guess so. Wow, I'm speechless right now. If this is true, I didn't see it coming," Maxi returned.

"Me neither. And I can't afford to lose my job. Not now," Melissa replied, distraught.

"I can't afford to lose mine either," Maxi said, slowly replaying her conversation with Nancy. *"I'll be reaching out to everyone for an update—especially you." What did she mean by "especially you"? Geez, am I getting laid off?*

"Well, that's all I know, and I wasn't sure if you had heard anything or knew about it. I know you talk to Nancy more than most of us," Melissa quizzed Maxi.

Keeping her composure, Maxi calmly replied, "No, no, Melissa. Nancy has not even hinted at it to me, so thanks for sharing. I am concerned too, but at this point, I don't know what any of us can do but keep doing our jobs and, if we have a fallback plan, pull it out. Otherwise, we'd better start building one."

"Yeah, I don't have a fallback plan. I guess you're right, though. I better get back to work," Melissa said as she turned and exited the office.

*Oh, my goodness! I did not see that coming. We have this mortgage, and we're just getting comfortable in our home. I don't know what we will do if I lose this job. I hope this isn't real, and it's just some crazy rumor that goes away.*

Though she tried hard to convince herself that it was a rumor, Maxi grew increasingly concerned. If Melissa's story was true, it would be a shocker. Sure, she knew there had been a downturn in the client base, and there was talk about ramping up marketing and acquisition. Still, she did not think overall expenses and liabilities were such that the company had to make drastic cuts even before mid-year rolled around.

34

Maxi continued working and worrying through the afternoon with no disruptions or new fires to put out. Nancy had been extremely quiet all day. She had not even reached out to Maxi for a debriefing of the activities that occurred while she was on vacation. That made Maxi even more concerned about the layoff rumor. She had chatted with a few coworkers during and after the marketing meeting. Other than Melissa, no one had brought up the layoff rumor. Maxi always tried to steer clear of office gossip, so she kept the information to herself.

Overall, the business day had been relatively normal. Then the phone rang, and the caller ID displayed Nancy's office. *I guess she's finally out from under her emails. At least, I hope that's it and nothing else. Please, please, no layoffs!*

"Hi, Nancy," Maxi answered, focusing on her tone, not wanting to sound nervous.

"Hi, Maxi. Please meet me in the conference room next to my office."

"The conference room?"

"Yes, unless you're working on an escalation."

"No, no. I can meet you. Do I need to bring anything in particular, a report? Or do you want a summary of what happened or what came up while you were out?" Maxi asked.

"No, no. We will debrief later or tomorrow. Just bring yourself right now."

Maxi put the receiver down, raising her eyebrow. That was curious. *Just bring me. She doesn't want to debrief. Uh-oh. What's this all about? I sent her an email about the bank error. It wasn't on our end. It most certainly wasn't my doing.*

*And it's pretty well taken care of. No, it can't be that I'm getting laid off. What am I going to do? Okay, let me not go crazy trying to figure out what she wants beforehand. I'll handle it—whatever it is!*

As Maxi walked into the conference room doorway, she realized that she was not alone—it appeared that everyone else on Nancy's staff was there. Gloria, the secretary, was there. Tom, the programmer/statistician, was there. Victoria, the accounts payable assistant, was there. Sally, the accounts receivable assistant, was there. Oh, no. One person was missing: Melissa.

Maxi smiled apprehensively at everyone as she took her seat, then watched the confused expressions when Nancy closed the door and began to speak. Tom interrupted Nancy to ask the question on Maxi's mind and everyone else's: "Aren't you going to wait for Melissa?"

"No, she will not be attending."

A look of concern came over everyone's face as Nancy continued speaking.

"The firm is experiencing difficult financial times. The market and our client base are dwindling. While efforts are underway to boost the business and add new portfolios, effective immediately, each department must work from a significantly reduced operating budget. Unfortunately, given the size of our department, our reduced budget translates into a reduced head count. Therefore, I had to cut a position. I had a tough decision because I had to choose to end someone's employment. I made what I believed was the best decision for the company, department, and staff. I assessed the required functions to keep the business running. I evaluated the required skill set for each function and position. As always, the business needs and client's requirements are the priority. Therefore, I based my decision on how this department can continue meetings its objectives with fewer staff members." Nancy sighed and paused for a few seconds. Then she continued, "This was a tough decision to make, and I know it will be tough for each of you, but I decided to let Melissa go."

Quietly, Maxi sighed with relief. Then paranoia kicked in; she could feel the sweat beading on her forehead and the back of her neck. Every eye seemed to have turned and stared directly at her. *Are they thinking what I'm thinking? It had to be between Melissa and me; we performed the same function and job responsibilities. I bet they're questioning why Melissa, who has been with the company for ten years, was the one to lose her job and not me, who has only been here two years.*

After delivering the news, Nancy did not field questions. Instead, she directed everyone to go about business as usual until she reached out individually to discuss any role or responsibility adjustments.

*Business as usual? How do you drop such a bombshell, refuse to take questions, and then say, oh, go about business as usual? Then again, I shouldn't be surprised. I knew there was a reason Nancy was in here at the crack of dawn, returning from vacation on a Thursday. Yeah, D-Day is usually on a Thursday before a Friday payday. The company typically makes layoff notifications on the Thursday before payday and cuts one big check with everything they think they owe you on Friday, then they never have to deal with you again.*

Maxi returned to her office and sat at her desk in a daze. The news wreaked havoc on her concentration. She wanted to leave immediately, go home, and start over tomorrow. Since she had come in early that morning, she had already put in her time. Maxi scanned her email for any new fires or concerns with making payments after the bank error. Nothing had come in. She packed her things and walked to the subway.

As Maxi arrived at the subway platform, she saw a familiar face. It was Melissa. Maxi almost called out to her but then stopped.

*What am I going to say? "I'm sorry. It should have been me." You can't fix it for her. And it could have been you. Just walk away, Max. There is nothing you can say to make her feel better right now. You should walk away!*

Flustered and nervous, Maxi exhaled, turned, and walked quickly to the other end of the platform, ensuring that the two would not end up in the same subway car. After a few minutes, a train pulled into the station. Maxi hopped on and found a seat. She leaned against the window. Alone in her thoughts, she bit her lip—thankful but sad. If the company had selected her during this layoff, it would have seriously impacted her life and family. Still, she couldn't shrug off her earlier conversation with Melissa. *I don't know why they had to downsize. I feel bad for her.*

As much as she tried, Maxi could not stop thinking about the look on Melissa's face in her office and on the subway platform. She closed her eyes, trying to focus on other matters and somehow quiet her growing anxiety. It didn't work, and she almost missed her stop.

CHAPTER
# FOUR

The escalator was still broken, and the day's heat and humidity hit Maxi with increased intensity. She squinted, trying to readjust her eyes, which she had kept closed for much of the train ride because of the blinding sunlight and her melancholy mood brought on by the day's event. As she made her way outside, Maxi reached for her sunglasses to protect her eyes from the sun but primarily to mask the sadness she couldn't erase.

Before she knew it, Maxi was about to take the front steps to her home. Then the sound of a car with a loud muffler caught her attention. Maxi looked down the block to the left in the direction of the noise.

*Uh? Excuse me, but did I see what I thought I saw?*

Maxi stopped in her tracks and steadied her sunglasses. Next, she focused her vision on the end of the block and then on the traffic coming toward her. *Yeah, here he comes.* She stopped at the bottom step as Gary slowly half-walked and half-jogged toward the house, a book bag on his shoulders and a basketball in his hand. But Maxi was more interested in the green sedan with the loud muffler moving in the same direction—the green sedan she knew she saw Gary exit on the corner.

She didn't recognize the car. She had never seen it before. But as the car slowly rolled past her, she again focused her sight, staring intently. She removed her sunglasses and practically locked eyes with the driver. She gasped. Her heart sank. If she had been hot before, now she was boiling. Maxi knew those eyes anywhere. She turned from the car toward Gary, now only a few steps away. Eyes bulging, heavily breathing, and temporarily at a loss for words, Maxi shook her head in disbelief.

Gary saw his mother watching the car and tried to ignore her look of dismay as he arrived at the spot where she stood waiting. Gary kissed her on the cheek and greeted her nervously, "Hi, Mom. You're home already?"

Maxi didn't acknowledge the kiss or the greeting. Instead, with one hand on her hip and the other tightly holding her purse, sunglasses, and briefcase, she stared hard and directly into Gary's eyes. "Why are you just getting home?"

"I'm sorry, Mom. I stayed behind for a little pick-up game. I should have let you know. I'm sorry."

"Who was in this pick-up game?

"A few guys. Guys, I know, and guys from school."

"Name them."

"Mom, why are you making a big deal? I'm sorry. Come on, let's go inside. I'll tell you in advance the next time I stay late or have a pick-up game," he replied calmly.

Maxi took a deep breath, ignored his comments, and continued, "I said name them!"

At this point, the green sedan, which had continued down the block, turned around and pulled along the curb just a few feet from where Gary and Maxi were standing.

"Maxine, Maxine. Can I talk to you a second?" the driver called out.

Maxi flashed an angry stare at the driver, ignored his request, glared at Gary, and continued speaking. "After you name them, tell me how you got home?"

Gary responded, bolstered by the driver's presence, "You already know how I got home."

Mouth agape, Maxi grabbed Gary's upper arm and slightly pushed him toward the steps. "Go inside. I'll deal with you in a minute!"

Upset, Gary was about to respond but caught a glimpse of the driver nodding at him to follow his mother's instructions. Gary ran up the steps but stopped at the porch, anxious to witness the pending exchange.

Walking as if she were in a trance, Maxi took a few steps to get closer to the sedan and the driver. Simultaneously, the driver exited the car and walked toward her. He looked pretty much the same, a bit thinner, a little older, but those gray-blue eyes didn't seem to sparkle anymore—they seemed icy or glassy—and now he was sporting a head full of cornrows.

*Sure enough, it's Devin. No wonder my son's been bothering me about getting cornrows and fighting against going to the barbershop. It all makes perfect sense.*

"Leave my son alone! Do you understand?" Maxi hollered.

41

"Your son? Maxine, I ain't feeding into that nonsense," Devin replied.

"Nonsense! Having *my* son sneak around and lie to *me* is *nonsense*? Well, here's the deal. Don't pick up my son anywhere. I don't want him in your car. I don't want him around you. He has big dreams, and I have big plans, and you are not about to mess them up! Go back to wherever you've been. Most importantly, don't ever pull up to my house uninvited, or else!"

"Or else what? Girl, you're acting crazy and stupid. Maxine, go inside. Don't make a scene. You don't own the street or the curb. I can drive by and park here daily if I want to! And you certainly didn't make him by yourself. That's my son too!" Devin declared.

"Whatever! Do you think I'm joking? You'll see. Test me!" Maxi answered with gritted teeth as she turned and marched up the steps, brushing back her hair that had somehow, in her fury, moved from where it was before—neatly tucked behind her earlobe—to now almost covering her right eye.

Gary scampered inside before she reached the porch. Maxi dropped her belongings and slumped down in the porch chair; she wasn't ready to go inside.

Maxi shook her head with disgust as Devin entered his car, made a hard U-turn, and drove off at high speed, brakes squealing and muffler groaning—then a *screech* followed by a loud *boom*!

*Fool. Nobody with any sense drives like that.* "That's why I don't want my son with you or in your car!" Maxi yelled, watching the car speed down the block.

Maxi had hoped to calm down before addressing Gary.

But, although she was still fuming, she didn't want to sit outside much longer. The heat and humidity were more than she could stand. *This behavior is right up Devin's alley — inciting a fight, walking away, and leaving someone else to deal with the fallout.* Remembering how Devin liked to stir up things should have prompted Maxi to get control of her escalating emotions. Instead, it only irritated her more. She gathered her belongings and stormed inside, shouting, "Gary!"

Gary ran down the stairs, still upset but more nervous than ever. "Yes, Mom."

"Listen and listen well! Don't you ever lie to me! Do you understand? I sent you to school. I didn't send you to hang out with that man!" she roared.

Gary stared at his mother. He was breathing heavily, chest heaving, and mouth pouting, but he did not respond.

"Do you hear me?" Maxi asked, speaking deliberately.

Gary still didn't respond.

"Likkle bwoy, ansa wen I tawk to yu," Maxi shouted, speaking in Jamaican patois as she tended to do whenever her anger got the best of her.

"I ain't no boy, Mom. I just wanted to see Dad. Is that so bad?" Gary quietly grumbled, breathing heavily as though his chest was about to explode.

Caring only about her feelings at the moment, Maxi continued, "If I sey its bad, den, it's bad. I am de parent, and yu do wat I sey. Dat's ow it werks. Pickney du wat parents tell dem an I didn't tell yu fi get in dat man's kyar."

"Mom, stop saying that, please! I knew you'd be upset, but you're making it seem like it's some crazy man off the street somewhere and not my dad," Gary answered, visibly upset.

"Go, go! Go upstairs. Go to your room. I can't deal with this right now," Maxi finished, confused and emotional.

Gary hesitated for a second, then turned and ran upstairs without saying another word. As Maxi heard his bedroom door slam, she dropped her purse, briefcase, and sunglasses on the floor, sat on the bottom step, put her head in her lap, and cried.

Maxi wasn't sure how long she sat on the step, but she finally mustered the energy to climb the stairs. Hearing the music coming from Gary's bedroom, she almost knocked at the door as she passed by. But then she hesitated, realizing she needed time to think and choose her words. It was good that Tony wasn't home because she was still in a whirlwind and wanted some quiet time to sort out her feelings. She had not intended to scream at Gary. She had to fix that, but she needed to take some time to reflect before approaching him or addressing the issue.

As she entered her beautiful new bathroom, Maxi exhaled while adding drops of lavender aromatherapy oil into the tub. She undressed and submerged her body in the warm water—it was just what she needed to remove the anxiety that had tumbled down on her like an avalanche. Slowly, she closed her eyes and focused her thoughts on the comforting warmth and the soothing scent of lavender.

Just as Maxi began to feel the tension release itself from her body, out of nowhere came a loud voice: "Max, Max, Max, where are you?" Tony was leaping up the stairs, two steps at a time.

Maxi did not want to answer; she needed this time of

calm and solitude. *Hopefully, he'll get it and leave me alone.* But persistent as he was, Tony rattled the doorknob while continuing to call out to her. "Max, I know you're in there. Why aren't you answering? Are you okay? Why did you lock the door?"

*Why did I lock the door? That's a simple answer—privacy, alone time. Duh!* Maxi looked up at the skylight, rolled her eyes, squirmed, and sighed before replying curtly, "Yes. I'm in here!"

"Well, open up," Tony begged.

"I'm in the tub!" Maxi replied loudly.

"Come on, you can get out for a second. I don't want to talk through the door."

"We'll talk later when I'm out of the tub," Maxi replied.

"Well, you still need to open up because I've got to go," answered Tony.

"Go use the other bathroom. That's why we invested in adding an extra bathroom," Maxi said defiantly.

"No, no, I need to use the one you're using because I want to see you and talk to you," answered Tony. "Come on. Baby, baby, baby, open the door," he pleaded.

Maxi remained silent, hoping he would stay away.

"Max, you're not opening the door?" asked Tony.

Still, Maxi did not answer. She hoped that he would get the message and leave her alone. Then, she heard it. The knob jiggled. Maxi watched with disbelief as the key inset rotated. The door opened, and Tony stood there smiling mischievously. Maxi's mouth dropped. She looked at him and shook her head with disgust.

"I can't believe you picked the lock. You know how to tick me off, don't you!"

Clueless as to why she was so angry, Tony smiled as he walked over to the tub. Maxi glared, splashed water at him, laid back in the tub, closed her eyes, and ignored him.

"Baby, calm down, chill out. Sometimes you have to loosen up and not take everything as seriously as you do. Have a sense of humor, will you?"

Maxi did not answer.

Tony sat on the tub's edge, reached into the water, and splashed some at Maxi.

Again, Maxi glared at him, shaking her head. "I can't believe you picked the lock, though. *Sheesh*, can you give me a bit of privacy? I don't know why I put up with you."

"Baby, you know I'm a little crazy, and you love me anyway, and that is all there is to it," Tony said glumly. Then he kissed her softly and said, "But you know something? I love you too!"

"You're a mess," said Maxi, softening her stare, although she still didn't crack a smile.

"What's the matter, though? You seem down or annoyed."

"I had a horrible day."

"Well, I'm all ears. What happened?" Tony asked, concerned.

"A lot. A whole lot," Maxi said with an attitude.

"I'm listening. Tell me, babe," Tony said as he squirmed to sit comfortably on the bathtub's edge.

Maxi knew he wouldn't leave until she told him every detail. Besides, she figured talking about it might help. She recounted the stressful events at the office, Devin's sudden resurfacing, and her attack (of sorts) on Gary.

Tony splashed his hand around in the water for several

seconds before responding.

"Well, baby, let's tackle the easy one first. You didn't get laid off. You've got your job. And you're good at what you do, and you know that don't you?" asked Tony. "Besides, you can't worry about who might say what about Melissa getting laid off and not you. Don't let potential whispers get to you; keep doing your thing, and your work will prove that they made the right decision to keep you. You still have to produce, or they'll let you go in a heartbeat. Just don't sweat it or worry about any comments or side-eyes at work, okay? Just do *you*! Stuff will happen. I remember my mom used to say, *"Son, you gonna get caught in a storm from time to time; instead of getting frightened or upset, sometimes you've gotta dance in the rain!"*

Tony splashed water at Maxi as he continued, "Dance, lady, dance!"

Maxi sighed and smiled slightly.

"But now that other thing. I will chill for right now. However, I know it's Gary's father, but he can't just pop up at our spot. That's going to be a real problem for me."

"I know that. It's a problem for me too!"

"Okay, but that aside, I love Gary. *He's my son.* And I will always be there for him, whatever he needs. The guy can't just pop up here when he wants to. But if Gary wants his father, I can't deny him that. I wish I had my father now. Gary is twelve, and I was twelve when they took my pops from me. I can't deny him his pops," Tony finished, his voice almost cracking.

"Tony, I'm sorry, baby. I love you, and I know you care about Gary."

They were quiet for a minute or two, looking at each

other, letting their eyes communicate their emotions.

"Now, the third thing," Tony said, snickering. "My lady, my love, one of the best moms I know, you can't talk to your son like that. You're going to have to clean that up. Fix it and fix it quickly."

"I know that too. Seeing that man and his glassy stare just made me flip out," she said, gritting her teeth.

"All right, relax. Calm down," Tony instructed, stroking her cheek.

"And he has cornrows, Tony. That's why Gary's been bugging me about cornrows," she continued, irritated.

"Max, I will say this to you. You need to fix it with your son. Don't get wired up and make it all about that dude. Think about your son. You can't go off getting all *Jamaican-mad* and calling the young man *bwoy* and *pickney*," he said, trying to imitate the patois dialect while shaking his head and chuckling.

"That was terrible. I can't believe I did that. But I did it. I have to own it," Maxi answered with a deep breath.

"Okay, I'll leave you alone and let you chill. Think about how to apologize to your son. Please don't make him go to bed mad at you, Max! And maybe later you should talk to Miz Leonie about the whole situation with his father. Your mom has been through some stuff. She might have some good advice."

"Yeah, I was thinking that too. Mom is always a good sounding board, although I bet she will probably say I should talk to his father, get straight on his son's needs, and set some ground rules. I'm sure Gary has his number, and I should probably speak with him. He can't pop in and out of my son's life according to his convenience."

"Yeah, *we* should talk with him."

"Tony, I don't think that's necessary."

"Max, it's very necessary. I understand his rights as a man and a father, but this is *my* family. I'm not going to start any foolishness. I merely want to meet him, because I think he should know who I am and where I'm coming from."

Maxi nods. "Okay, babe. We'll talk about that later."

"Yeah, I'll let you have your relaxation time. We can talk some more later or tomorrow. I'll let you have your *alone time.*"

"Okay, just fifteen more minutes, all right?"

Tony leaned in and kissed her lips, softly holding the lower portion before slowly pulling away.

Maxi let out a deep, comforting sigh, sliding down into the water, and stopping just before it reached her nostrils. *Hmm. Unplug your mind for these precious moments, Max. The storm will pass. Dance, dance, dance!*

Maxi did not want her disagreement with Gary to linger. She agreed with Tony. She could not let him go to bed, angry at her and confused about how to handle seeing his father. Maxi knew that was a recipe for trouble. After soaking in the tub, relaxing, reflecting, and reining in her feelings, she knocked on Gary's bedroom door. She had to knock several times and call out his name before he opened the door.

"Can I come in?" she asked softly.

Gary pulled the door open but didn't speak.

Maxi walked in and plopped down on his bean bag as she had done many times before. Gary sat at the edge of his bed.

Maxi stared up at Gary, nervous and holding back tears

as she spoke. "Gary, my son, you are a wonderful young man—not perfect, but I wouldn't trade you for anyone or anything. I was wrong. I was angry, but that was no excuse. I don't like what you did. But, Gary, I shouldn't have screamed and hollered. Baby, I am sorry. I don't want you to lie to me, and I don't want to give you a reason even to consider lying to me. The main thing is you're my son. My one and only baby *bwoy,* and I don't want to lose your love or harm our relationship," Maxi said softly.

"I'm not mad at you . . . anymore, Mom! I know sometimes you get *Jamaican-mad,* as Tony calls it," he answered. "But I'm all right."

They both chuckled.

"I know you weren't just trying to be mean," Gary continued. "I'm sorry too, Mom. I knew you'd be mad. But I still wanted to see Dad. He found out where I go to school from my cousin Manny, and he showed up after school a few months ago. He said he had moved back here."

"Moved back here. Where was he?" asked Maxi.

"He was in Florida for years, he said. We've just been playing ball and kicking it. He hasn't said anything bad about you or anything like that. We've just been talking about me, you know, what I've been doing and what I want to do. I like it, Mom. I'm glad he's back," Gary said, rambling.

"Hmm," answered Maxi, nodding understandingly, and restraining herself.

"You're not gonna stop me from seeing him are you, Mom?" Gary asked nervously.

Maxi sighed, stood up, and embraced her son. Gary hugged her in return.

"I want the best for you. I want you to be happy. We'll have to figure something out. I'll figure something out. You don't have to worry. Mom will take care of it," Maxi consoled him.

"Please, Mom. I have his number. You can call him," Gary pleaded.

"Okay. Okay. Put the number on the bulletin board downstairs," Maxi replied reassuringly. They locked in an embrace and remained that way until they heard Tony calling them for dinner.

After dinner and clearing the dishes, Tony and Gary headed to the basement. Another game was on television. It was the topic at the dinner table, and it helped to take everyone's mind off the day's commotion. While Tony and Gary were glued to the TV, Maxi grabbed the cordless phone, walked to the living-room sofa, curled up under a light, summer cotton quilt, and dialed.

"Hello."

"Hi, Mom. How are you?" Maxi asked.

"Hi, Max. I'm fine, baby girl. What's the matter?" Leonie questioned.

"Why do you think something is the matter?" Maxi responded.

"Max, I carried you for nine months and raised you; I can tell when there is the slightest twitch, tremble, stutter, or change in your voice. What's going on?" Leonie demanded.

Maxi chuckled nervously. "He's back, Mom. Devin is back from wherever. Gary says it's Florida. And he's been sneaking around, picking my son up from school, and having him hide it and lie to me!"

"Hmm."

"Hmm. Mom, is that all you're going to say? *Hmm?*" Maxi asked.

"Max. I don't particularly appreciate that he has Gary lying to you. But can you hear the high pitch in your voice when you say, "my son"? You didn't make him by yourself. And, if Gary has been going with him, hiding, and telling you lies, it means he wants to spend time with his father. I'm not going to tell you what to do, but I'm going to tell you don't make it, so you push your son to Devin and away from you!" Leonie counseled her daughter.

"Yeah, I guess I know that. I have to confess to you. I went off on Gary. I went *Jamaican-mad,* did the whole *bwoy* and *pickney* thing," she said, laughing.

"Maxi, no, you didn't!" exclaimed Leonie.

"Mom, yes, I did. But we talked, and I apologized, and we're back good," Maxi answered.

"Well, it's good you didn't let that fester. But don't do that again. And this is why you need to handle the situation quickly because you don't want to push Gary to the other side," Leonie replied.

Maxi took a deep breath before continuing. "I know. I will set up a meeting with Devin so we can talk and come to some agreement. Hopefully, we can clear the air and set a standard for how we interact and when he sees and spends time with Gary, although I don't know why Gary wants anything to do with him. After my father had been gone for a few years, I moved on. I didn't want to see him. I still wouldn't want to see him if he showed up now. I washed him out of my hair and my life!"

"Well, Max, that is you, not Gary," said Leonie.

"If my father reached out to you today, Mom, would you talk to him?" asked Maxi.

A few seconds of silence filled the air.

"I might, Max. I might. I would be cordial and let him see that I have more than survived without him. I don't think I would be hateful, though, just firm. I wouldn't start a friendship, but one conversation wouldn't be bad," Leonie confirmed.

"Well, if he ever reaches out and asks for me, tell him I'm dead!" Maxi said with disdain.

"Maxine Desiree Weldon, watch what you say. It's that attitude that makes you go off on people. Besides, you're not Gary. You can't make him feel what you want him to feel or want what you want. Be careful lest you lose him while trying to hold on too tight," Leonie advised.

"All right, all right, Mom, I know what I have to do," Maxi said.

"Okay, dear. Be kind and put your son's needs first, you hear?"

"I will, Mom. Have a good night. We'll talk soon," said Maxi.

"Okay, baby. Love you."

"Love you too, Mom. Bye now."

Maxi laid the phone on her chest, pondering whether she was ready to make this phone call. After some ten minutes of wrangling back and forth in her mind, she walked to the hallway's bulletin board and dialed the number Gary had posted on it.

"Hey!" came a voice at the other end.

*See what I'm saying? He can't even say hello when he answers the phone like you're supposed to.* "Good evening. May I speak with Devin, please?" asked Maxi.

"Hey, Maxine. You know it's me," Devin answered.

"Actually, I didn't," replied Maxi, although she did.

"Oh, now you don't recognize my voice," Devin continued.

Maxi looked up at the ceiling, grinding her teeth, and took a deep breath before she spoke.

"Devin, let me get to the reason for this call. I think, no, I *know* we need to talk. It's about Gary. We need to get on the same page with what's best for him and how we will interact."

"I'm all ears. Go ahead," Devin said curtly.

"I'd like to talk in person. I think what we have to discuss requires more than a phone call," she replied.

"All right, I can do that. I'm easy," Devin answered.

*I would respond to that "easy" comment, but this is about Gary's needs. Max, behave yourself!*

"Tomorrow? Friday. Evening. Around six. I don't want this to linger. We can meet at that eatery across from Howard University. It's walking distance from here, but I'm not sure if that's convenient for you," Maxi responded.

"Naw. I can't do Friday," Devin replied.

Silence. Maxi took a deep breath. "Okay, I thought you were *easy*. Nevertheless, when can you meet?" Maxi asked with sarcasm.

"I *am* easy. But I have something scheduled for Friday evening. How about Saturday in the afternoon around lunchtime? You know, twelve or one o'clock?" he suggested.

"Okay, now *I'm* easy. I can do that. Let's say twelve-thirty," Maxi replied, needing to feel empowered by selecting the exact time.

"All right, twelve-thirty is cool. Where are we meeting then?" asked Devin.

"Well, I had suggested the eatery across from Howard University if that's not too much trouble for you," Maxi continued, annoyed.

"All right, all right. I'm good with that," replied Devin.

"Great. Now, in the meantime, could you refrain from picking up my son, Gary, after school?" asked Maxi.

"I'll meet you Saturday afternoon, Maxine, to talk about *our* son," Devin responded with an attitude.

Maxi rolled her eyes. "Okay, I'll see you then," she said, clicking the "off" button on the receiver without formally saying goodbye.

*Ay, ya, yi. He's not going to make this easy, and Tony wants to come to the meeting. This is insane!*

JACQUELINE P. WALKER

# CHAPTER
# FIVE

Maxi knocked on Gary's door and poked her head in the room before heading off on her Friday morning commute. She wanted to ensure they were back on good terms and that he still wasn't upset.

"Morning. Get up, dear, and don't be late for school," she said sweetly.

"Morning, Mom. I'm getting up in a few minutes. I won't be late. Have a good day, okay?" Gary answered, stretching and yawning.

"Okay, you too," Maxi said, reaching down to pull the doorknob.

Then Gary called out, "Mom, I'm going to meet Dad again today, okay? I told you I wouldn't lie anymore."

Maxi hesitated but noticed his pleading eyes. "Okay, I'm getting with him in the next few days. I promised I would work it out, and I will," she informed him.

"You are? When? Which day?" Gary asked, sitting up in bed, appearing partly afraid and partly excited.

Maxi smiled softly. "Yes, I told you I would, and I am true to my word. Don't worry; we'll work it all out. I'm going to make it happen before next week, okay? I promise we'll be all squared away by next week," Maxi answered.

"Thanks, Mom. I love you," Gary said with a big smile.

"I love you, son. See you later," Maxi replied, smiling back at him.

Maxi ran down the steps and greeted Tony, who was munching on his usual giant bowl of cereal. She shook her head and chuckled.

"What's so funny?" he asked.

"Nothing funny, just a cheerful sight for my eyes," Maxi answered, planting a kiss on his cheek. "Gary is just getting up. If you're getting out early this morning, please check on him before you leave," she continued.

"I've got him. No worries," Tony replied.

"Oh, I relented and said it was okay for him to see his father again today. I'm just letting you know if you get home early and he's not around," Maxi commented.

"All right, when will we see him?" asked Tony.

"Excuse me? See him?" Maxi asked, pretending she didn't understand what Tony was asking.

Annoyed, Tony clarified, "When are you going to make that phone call and set up a meeting with his father?"

"Oh, that. Well, I called last night," replied Maxi.

Surprised, Tony asked, "When were you going to tell me?"

"You guys were watching the game or whatever, and

then I didn't feel like discussing it before bed," Maxi responded.

"Okay, but you weren't volunteering the information this morning. I had to ask. But again, when were you going to tell me?" Tony repeated with disbelief.

"Tony, I would have told you later this evening. I didn't want to have this conversation before work. I have enough stress with that," Maxi said, searching for an excuse.

"Well, we're already talking about it. I think we might as well continue the discussion. When are *we* meeting? You didn't answer that part," Tony continued.

"*I* am meeting with him Saturday afternoon. I don't want to make this a big deal, so I don't need to pull you into this," Maxi replied.

"*Pull me into this?* Max, what's gotten into you? This exchange right here and now ain't how we've ever dealt with anything since we been together. And yeah, let's address it. I know Gary ain't my biological son, but based on the relationship I've built with him and you, you're going to tell me there's *no need to pull me into this?*" Tony asked, irritated.

"Tony, you know that's not what I meant," she answered.

"No, I don't know because that's what you said loud and clear," Tony shot back, raising his voice.

"Okay, Tony, let's not get into an argument about this, especially with Gary upstairs. We'll talk later," Maxi said.

Tony shook his head but didn't say a word.

"Hey, I love you," Maxi responded as she walked over and planted a kiss on his lips.

Tony showed no reaction to her affection but replied, "I love you too, Max, but I don't like how you're acting this morning."

"We'll talk. Have a great day. I love you," Maxi answered, hugging him.

"I love you, Max. Go on and have a good day," Tony answered, kissing her forehead, though it was clearly more an act of courtesy than affection at that moment.

Maxi let go of Tony and waved as she walked toward the front door, smiling sweetly with her eyes. But Tony reacted only by flashing the peace sign with his fingers as she closed the door and skipped down the front steps.

Upon arriving at the office, Maxi pulled the mirrored door to enter the lobby, bracing herself for the fallout from the previous day's events and news. Because she knew she was always the first one in, Maxi wasn't expecting anyone else to be there unless Nancy was an early bird again. But no surprises today; there wasn't a person in sight, no open office doors, and no light in any cubicle. Maxi had to hit the light switch after exiting the elevator and opening the floor's access door. Nancy's office was dark and quiet. Maxi headed straight to her office, turned on her computer, and prepared for the day.

The bank had sent an update. They had processed repayments for most of the transactions impacted by the error. The final two were in progress and were expected to be completed by the day's end. Maxi breathed a sigh of relief. Then she noticed Nancy's email: a request for a one-on-one meeting later in the day at two o'clock. *I guess this is when she tells me what additional responsibilities I have to pick up. But I know one thing for sure, if the company thinks I'm taking on Melissa's entire portfolio plus mine at the same level and pay grade, I've got news for them. I don't care what kind of financial trouble they claim to have; I'm not doing two jobs for one paycheck. Yeah, I need the money, but there's a point where you have to draw the line.*

The day progressed uneventfully but slowly and with a persistent feeling of melancholy. Everyone seemed to mumble polite greetings without looking each other in the eye. Smiles, light exchanges, and informal chats were non-existent. This layoff was the second Maxi had experienced since being employed at the firm. She was getting used to the change in the atmosphere after a layoff, which lingered for weeks before returning to normal.

Then to boot, there was the thing with Devin and the other thing with Tony. Maxi did not want Tony at the meeting with Devin. She knew Devin's modus operandi—imply and instigate. Likewise, she knew her husband's style—support his wife and never back down.

*I'm not going to start a fight or ongoing conflict that pushes Gary away from me or makes him think Tony might persuade me to keep him from his father. I want my son to be happy. I want him to continue the great relationship he's built with Tony these past years. And, if he really wants his father, I'll consent to it. But if he decides otherwise, I won't be the one trying to convince him to do so. Life! When it rains, it pours, doesn't it? And I don't care what Tony says—I don't feel like dancing today. He didn't sound like he did, either. He didn't even call me today. He could have called to say hey and reassure me, given it's the day after layoffs. I would have told him about the meeting with Nancy and run my thoughts and plans by him. But nothing. Geez. I could call, but I don't need the tension right now. I'll figure this out by myself and deal with Tony later.*

A few minutes before two, Maxi grabbed a notepad for her meeting. As she approached Nancy's office, the door opened, and another staff member exited, glancing at Maxi and giving her a stiff nod before quickly walking down the hallway.

*Uh. New assignment revolving door. I guess everyone is getting their marching orders!*

"Come on in, Maxi. Have a seat."

"Thanks, Nancy."

"How are you today?"

"I'm doing okay."

"Just, okay?"

"Yeah, just okay."

Nancy searched Maxi's expression for a clue to her true feelings. Finding nothing of genuine concern, she initiated the planned conversation regarding duties after the layoff announcement.

"Listen Maxi, I know the announcements probably shook you. But don't be afraid; I believe the company's steps will put us on a solid foundation for a while. Job loss shouldn't be your concern. But, of course, being one head down, there will be plenty of work."

Nancy laughed nervously. Maxi pursed her lips, but her facial expression did not change.

"All right, here's the deal, Maxi. With Melissa gone, I primarily need your help with her portfolio," Nancy said bluntly.

"What does that mean? What type of help do you expect from me?" Maxi asked, matching Nancy's tone.

"I don't expect you to do it all. I'll be helping too, but you have the most similar experience. Also, the payables and receivables staff, Sally, and Victoria have some availability, ability, and interest in learning more. I thought I'd put you over them like a team lead of sorts, and then you can train them to help with Melissa's old portfolio and even yours. That way, they will develop new skill sets, and you will get an opportunity to gain supervisory experience. Then we will have a team that can cover multiple functions, you know, when people take vacations, etc.," Nancy rambled on, seemingly presenting a mandate rather than a request to Maxi.

Suddenly, it dawned on Maxi that this may very well be her golden opportunity! The company had a plan. Nancy seemed to have a plan. Why shouldn't *she* have a plan? Maybe she could turn the tables in her favor. *I am not stupid; I know the drill. They let Melissa go. If I leave voluntarily, they're not going to crawl and ask Melissa to come back to fill the void. And they won't quickly find someone who already understands their specific operating procedures or is familiar with their client base. Everyone is replaceable, including me. But, at least for a while, they need my knowledge, work ethic, and proven ability to collaborate, build working relationships, and achieve exceptional results. No one else in this department knows enough to get this done without some training and ramp-up time. While I have this window of opportunity, I shouldn't just give in to their demands. But what's the limit? How far should I push?*

Maxi responded in a slow, deliberate, soft, but slightly sarcastic tone, "Okay, let me make sure that I understand.

63

I get to be a 'team lead of sorts.' I get increased responsibility and workload. I get to train staff. I get to supervise staff. And I get all this at my same level and pay grade."

"Well, Maxi, come on. You see the potential for you to advance out of this as time allows. With the layoffs and company position, we couldn't promote you and increase your salary right now. How would that look?" asked Nancy.

Maxi stared at her without responding.

"Maxi, we could say you're the acting manager. You know that means when the annual review period comes around, you will be officially set to get the manager title based on your performance, which I am certain will be exceptional. Then your job classification and pay grade will change, and you will get a substantial salary increase," Nancy said encouragingly.

Maxi chuckled. She was a bit nervous but determined. *This is a unique situation, and I'm taking a great chance. But since I've been with the company, they've made special arrangements for others under exceptional circumstances. Why can't they do the same for me?*

"Nancy, we are just coming up on mid-year. What I am hearing is I would have to wait at least six more months before getting any tangible benefit. But I would have significantly more tasks and, certainly, many more responsibilities, which would translate into more hours, more stress, and less work-life balance. I know you've got to give up something to get something, right? Hence, I am willing to make sacrifices but within reason and with some level of compensation," Maxi answered with humble confidence.

"Hmm. Okay, Maxi, tell me, what would you propose?" Nancy asked slowly and deliberately.

Maxi knew this was her opportunity to go after what she wanted. *When they don't throw you out of their office, and they ask you what you propose, that's your opening. Seize it!*

She cleared her throat and delivered her demands keeping her tone calm and professional but firm. "Okay, Nancy. I don't want you merely to *say* I am the "acting manager." You can officially change my title without changing my pay. I understand if you won't upgrade my salary right now, although you probably could." She chuckled nervously. "Still, if you're unwilling to upgrade my salary, but you officially change my title to a classification in the manager category, then that new job classification will drive the amount of every bonus I get for the remaining quarters this year. That means I'll at least get a little extra before the end-of-year reviews. Then after the end-of-year reviews, you can officially upgrade my salary and remove the 'acting' from my title that way I will get the full benefit of a manager's title based on my performance. I think that's fair and doable."

Nancy took a deep breath, then responded, "You drive a hard bargain, Maxi. I have to run it up the executive management chain."

"Of course. I understand," answered Maxi.

"Okay, it's Friday afternoon. I'll see if I can get an answer today. But it may very well have to wait until Monday. I'll let you know either way," Nancy replied.

"Okay, thanks for considering it. I'll wait to hear back," Maxi said.

Nancy nodded. Maxi knew that meant the meeting was over. She gathered her notebook and walked back to her office. *It will be okay. They were testing me to see if I would take the crumbs. Otherwise, she wouldn't even be taking my proposal to anyone. I probably should have demanded more. But no sense in being greedy right now. Small steps. Just don't settle for crumbs. A slice of bread will do for now, even if you can't get the whole sandwich. I think that's like dancing in the rain, right?*

Maxi settled down and focused on assembling as much as possible for the upcoming mid-year reports. She knew getting the baseline done would put her in good shape, especially since she would likely be required to do the same for Melissa's portfolio, plus all the new impending duties. Just as Maxi was getting mired in the reports, the phone rang.

"Hi, Nancy," Maxi said, appearing calm, although she was eager to hear Nancy's response to her request.

"Hey, Maxi. Listen, sorry," Nancy said.

"Sorry?" Maxi asked, concerned.

"No, no, no. Sorry, I can't get an answer today. Tom left early. But I'll get to him first thing on Monday, okay?" Nancy clarified.

"Oh, okay, Monday is fine," Maxi answered, relieved.

"Well, you have a good weekend, and we will touch base on Monday," Nancy replied.

"Thanks, Nancy. Have a great weekend. Bye now," said Maxi.

*It was already going to be a long weekend without having to wait until Monday for a decision from Nancy. This delay is just one more thing hanging over my head. I still need to work out this meeting with Devin. I still don't want Tony there, but I don't want a rift growing between Tony and me. Our conversation this morning wasn't typical for us. It was tense and not playful like it usually is. Tony got quite somber and seemed offended. We must fix that somehow, but I don't know how to do it right now.*

JACQUELINE P. WALKER

# CHAPTER
# SIX

Friday afternoon commutes were always a bear. All the way home, Maxi's mind raced back and forth. She wasn't sure how to approach the conversation with Devin. And she was growing increasingly unsure of how to handle things with Tony.

*The peace sign Tony gave me on my way to work seemed dismissive. Ugh. I cannot believe this is how I'm starting a weekend— with turmoil! This Tony thing. Then there's the Gary thing. I only want Gary to be happy, to stay out of trouble, and to have opportunities to make something positive out of his life. And the Tony thing and the Gary thing stem from the Devin thing! I don't know what Devin wants. I expect that he wants to spend time with Gary and hopefully rebuild their relationship. I hope he will have enough sense to begin offering financial support. But demanding child support is not my primary goal. If he is going to be in Gary's life, he has to be consistent. He can't disappear when he feels like it for as long as he wants.*

As the crowded train, bursting with chatter, approached the station, Maxi bristled at the thought of facing the boiling hot sun and dripping humidity. She barely escaped being mowed down by a fellow commuter as she took a quick second to exhale and prepare to face the elements before heading up the still-broken escalator. After safely reaching the top of the escalator, Maxi stepped out into the blazing heat and quickened her stride, sweating and panting. Today, more than ever, she was relieved when she opened her home's front door and felt the cool air flowing evenly from the air conditioner. *Uh, that's what I'm talking about! Thank you, Jesus, for your small mercies. It's brutal out there.*

Hearing movement and rustling, she walked back toward the kitchen, and Gary greeted her, smiling as he dug inside a bag of potato chips.

"Hi, Mom! How was your day?" he asked, kissing her on the cheek.

"It was fine, Mr. Potato Chips. How was yours?" she asked.

"It was good. It's Friday. Friday is always good," he answered, grinning.

"Hmm. I hope you did your homework or have a plan to get it done before Sunday, right?" she answered, smirking.

"I do, Mom. I know. I'm not going to wait until the last minute," he replied.

"Okay, sir. Is Tony here?" Maxi asked.

"Yeah, he's downstairs. We were waiting on you to see what you wanted to do this evening," Gary continued.

"Me? What did you all decide? I know you two. You act

like I have a choice when you all already have a plan," she said sarcastically.

"Naw. No way, Mom. We have some ideas, but we were waiting on you," he said.

"Tell me, what are the ideas that you've already settled on?" Maxi asked.

"See, Mom. You're trying to twist me up. I'll wait for Tony to answer that one," Gary said, digging into the bag of chips again.

"Well, if that's what you want to do. But don't stuff yourself on those chips unless that's what you all decided on for dinner," Maxi said with a scolding eye roll.

"It's just a quick snack since we're not going until about seven or seven-thirty," he said before realizing that he had let most of their plan slip.

"You all were waiting on me, but you already know that we're going around seven or seven-thirty...hmm," she commented.

"Ah, Mom, that's just the time. We haven't picked the place yet," he answered, tapping his forehead in disbelief at his blunder.

"No worries. I will be upstairs when someone cares to tell me what our *family* activity is for the night," Maxi responded curtly, walking past the basement door, and taking the stairs up to the main bedroom.

Potato chips in hand, Gary ran downstairs to warn Tony.

"Max, Max," Tony called out, taking the steps two at a time and making his typical loud entrance into the bedroom.

"Hey, Tony."

"Hey, I didn't know you were here," he said, walking over and tapping her butt as she got out of her work clothes and pulled on a T-shirt.

"I am here," she said abruptly.

"What's wrong with you?" he asked, attempting to kiss her just before she slightly turned her head, leaving his lips to gather a bundle of her hair.

"Okay, that's how it is?" Tony replied, annoyed and brushing hair out of his mouth.

Maxi did not respond.

"What's up, Max? This isn't like you. What's up with the attitude?" Tony asked, annoyed.

"Nothing's up," Maxi answered.

"Are you upset because you think we made plans without your input?" Tony asked, twisting his face and shrugging his shoulders. "Who are you? Because that's not my Max. Come on," he said, taking her hand and leading her to the edge of the bed. Tony sat down and patted the space next to him, beckoning her to do the same.

"So, what's up, Max? Seriously?" he asked. "You know I'm not the kind to hold stuff, get ticked off at the smallest thing, and walk around not talking to you, and you've never been like that. Please tell me what this is all about because I know it isn't because we decided we wanted to go bowling before you had a chance to agree or disagree. It isn't as though this is the first time, we've planned something before you got home," he finished.

"Uh, so that's it, bowling. You two decided you want to go bowling, which is not on my list of favorites," Maxi replied.

"Let's be serious, Max. There isn't too much you would

have come up with alone. You want to read, watch a movie, or go to eat. I can't think of much more," Tony answered, snickering.

"See what I mean? Go do what you all want to do," she answered, attempting to stand and walk away, but she could not escape Tony's grip as he was still holding her hand.

Maxi sat back down quietly, looking straight ahead. *I thought I was coming home to try and smooth things out; somehow, I've fueled the flame. Their decision to go bowling or do whatever shouldn't have gotten under my skin like this. But it did!*

The two sat quietly for a few seconds, although it seemed forever.

"Hey, Max. Let's be real. Maybe this whole thing about going to meet with Devin has gotten you wired and sensitive. Maybe it's gotten me like that a little bit, too," Tony said, reinitiating the conversation.

"Okay, yeah. Tony, you gave me the peace sign as a parting greeting this morning. The peace sign!" she answered, speaking deliberately.

"Well, peace is a good thing, right?" Tony answered, chuckling as Maxi sighed with disbelief. "Okay, all right. I did, and it wasn't the thing to do. But, Max, how do you decide if I shouldn't or can't go with you to meet this guy? Like, what am I? Your sidekick or your husband?" Tony asked sarcastically.

"Aha! So, since I decided to go alone to meet with Devin, you figured you'd decide to go bowling or whatever without considering me," Maxi replied, annoyed.

"Max let's leave that silly bowling thing out because you

know that ain't got nothing to do with this. We're talking about the meeting with Gary's father," Tony responded calmly.

Maxi pursed her lips as if unwilling to speak.

"So, what time are we meeting him, where are we meeting him, and let me clearly understand your position? What do you want?" Tony asked.

"Tony, I know how Devin is. He loves confrontations—they energize him! And I know how you are—you think you need to protect and defend me to the utmost," Maxi replied.

"Max. You didn't answer the question. You told me what you wanted me to hear, but you didn't tell me what I wanted to hear," Tony said without raising his voice.

*Yeah, I didn't answer. But I know Tony, and I know Devin. They don't know each other. But I know them both, so I know what will happen, and I can't let it happen. I'm not answering him. At least not right now.*

Tony chuckled, closed his eyes, and held his forehead before speaking. "See, Max, here's the thing. If you think there's going to be a confrontation, then who better to protect you than your husband?" Tony asked, staring intently at Maxi.

Maxi stared back silently.

"And, Max, I know you know me. Of course, you know I'll protect and cover you. But don't you know that I'm not stupid? I'm not out bucking for a fight. Max, this isn't about you, me, or that man. It's about that young man downstairs waiting for us. You know what, Max? I'm going to let you sleep on it. Besides, I need to hit some pins right now and don't want to keep Gary waiting or wondering. Stay home!" he said coolly, letting go of her hand, exiting the bedroom, and bounding down the stairs as loudly as he went up. "Gary, Gary, you ready? Let's go! If I win the first game, you've gotta wash my car!"

CHAPTER
# SEVEN

axi was up by seven o'clock on Saturday morning. Her stomach was growling, and she had a headache, but she still didn't want anything to eat. She hadn't had a meal since lunch on Friday, but she wasn't rushing to change that—she was hungry and full simultaneously. Tony was still asleep, looking happy in "Snoresville." Maxi heard when he and Gary came in last night, but she pretended to sleep because she wasn't ready to face Tony. Now the morning was here. There were chores and, of course, the big event: a twelve-thirty meeting with Devin. *If he even remembered and showed up. Maybe, I should call and remind him. Hmm, no, Max. It would help if you left well enough alone.*

After a cup of tea, Maxi started her chores. She decided to clean up downstairs first and do some laundry. She was dragging and not entirely up to it, but keeping busy gave her spurts of relief from thinking about the drama. She might consider making breakfast when the "bowlers" showed signs of life. It would be her apology without uttering a word. But right now, her headache was enough reason not to volunteer for that effort. She was in the basement sorting clothes when she heard Gary call out, "Mom, Mom, are you down here?"

"Hey, Gary, what's the matter?" Maxi asked, sticking her head out of the entrance to the laundry room.

"Can I go to the park with my friends?" he asked.

"What time?" she questioned.

"About eleven?" Gary responded.

"Okay. Strip your bed and bring me the sheets. Then clean your room, including making the bed, and you need to have breakfast before you jet off to play basketball," Maxi said. "Oh, do you know if Tony is up?" she added, glancing at the clock on the wall. It was almost eight-thirty.

"He's up. He's in the kitchen. He said he was about to make breakfast," Gary answered, running back upstairs.

"Oh, okay," Maxi replied, a bit surprised. She grimaced a bit at the thought of facing Tony because she wasn't sure what to say after how their conversation had ended last evening. But her gut told her to face the problem head-on now instead of letting it linger. The meeting with Devin was a mere four hours away, and although she didn't want Tony there, she wanted that feeling of comfort and support that she was so used to having from him. Maxi sighed, placed the laundry on the counter, and headed for the kitchen.

"Morning. I thought you were still asleep," she said to Tony, courteously but aloof.

"Good morning. I'm up. I got breakfast going. Any special requests?" Tony asked begrudgingly.

"No, no special requests. But I can help," Maxi offered.

"If you want to," Tony responded, shrugging his shoulders.

"Okay, well, you've got bacon going, so I'll get some eggs," Maxi said, taking charge.

"That's cool," Tony answered calmly.

The two went about making breakfast and setting the table with minimal conversation.

Gary took his laundry to the basement, then sat with Tony and Maxi for breakfast.

There wasn't much said except for grace until Gary spoke up.

"Hey, Tone, don't forget you owe me," he said, grinning with pride.

"Ah, man, you know that was a lucky strike, right?" Tony replied with a chuckle.

"Naw, you know that wasn't luck. I was killing it all night," Gary said.

"I'll admit it was your night. Your *lucky* night. How about we go double or nothing?" Tony asked.

"What?" Gary asked, confused.

"Well, instead of paying out your winnings, let them ride. Then, if you win again next week, I owe you double for both weeks. But, if I win, then we wipe it all out, and I don't owe you nothing," Tony proposed.

"I guess bowling is on tap again next week?" Maxi interjected.

"Yeah, we had a great time," Tony answered, mocking her question. "Hey, young man, what do you say to my wager?" he continued, looking directly at Gary.

"Yeah, Mom, we did have a great time, and I did promise

Tony a rematch. Are you going to come with us next week?" Gary asked, searching his mother's face for approval.

"Oh, that's fine. Probably," Maxi responded with a fake smile.

"Are you accepting the wager?" Tony asked, ignoring Maxi.

"I don't know, Tony. You might have some trick up your sleeve," Gary replied.

"I'm hurt. Don't you trust me? Come on now. You said it wasn't luck. Now you can have a big payday," he said, coaxing Gary.

"What did you win?" Maxi asked, trying to get in on the conversation.

"Tickets for me and a friend to go to the movie of my choice. Money for popcorn and a drink—and a ride, of course," Gary rambled.

"I see, and when is this?" she asked.

"Oh, when I square it away with you," Gary replied, slightly nervous.

"Cool, just let me know so you can collect your prize," Maxi replied, staring at Tony.

Tony looked down at his plate, seemingly engrossed in a slice of bacon and ignoring Maxi's comment.

"Thanks, Mom! Can I be excused? I need to finish reading a few chapters before I go to the park, so I won't have to do it later or tomorrow," Gary asked, looking directly at Maxi.

"Yes, you may," Maxi replied.

"Okay, run on out, afraid to accept my wager, I see," Tony said, waving Gary out.

"Naw, you just sprung it on me. I have to think about it,

man. I have to think about it," Gary begged.

"Okay, okay. I give you till midnight Sunday," Tony said, laughing.

"All right, you're laughing, but if I take it, you better be ready to pay up," Gary replied, running from the kitchen.

Tony chuckled. "I love that kid," he said, looking at Maxi.

Maxi didn't respond. She was a mess right now—fighting with Tony and anticipating fighting with Devin. She couldn't take another bite of food but continued sipping on her cup of tea.

On the other hand, Tony put another helping on his plate, apparently determined to keep his mouth full to avoid saying a word to Maxi.

She couldn't take it any longer. "Remember I have that twelve-thirty meeting," she said curtly.

"Oh, I remember. Did you tell Gary?" Tony asked.

"Not specifically. He knows I was planning to meet with his dad, but I didn't tell him it was today. But I don't know if Devin told him—Gary hasn't said anything to I assume he had sense enough not to. Anyway, he is going to the park at eleven, and he doesn't need to have that on his mind," she continued.

"Just wondering," Tony answered.

"Tony is this what we're going to do?" asked Maxi.

"What?" asked Tony, confused.

"Be dismissive and put up a wall. A wall of ice between us?" Maxi blurted out.

Tony placed his fork on the plate, finished chewing, swallowed, and then, staring directly at Maxi, said, "Max, I'm not being dismissive. That's you deciding I can't go with you to this meeting. And, as for the wall of ice, that's you getting mad about us not getting your approval to go bowling, jabbing me subtly with your words and your stare. Listen, go to your meeting, and work it out for Gary (I want you to). But remember, you have to come home. You have to come home. And we can't just close our eyes and make the wall of ice melt."

"Ouch, that was deep," Maxi answered, annoyed.

"Hmm. Deep, huh?" Tony said, frustrated, as he stood and reached for his plate so he could leave the table.

"Tony, please sit. Don't leave," Maxi said, noticing his expression.

"Why, Max? Why? You know I'm not much for arguments. But I do stand for what I believe, and I believe I should go with you," he said, placing both hands squarely on the table and staring directly at Maxi.

"Okay, okay. I don't want to fight. I don't like this uncomfortable feeling between us. You can go with me to the meeting," Maxi said in a tone of surrender.

Tony sat. "Maxi, are you changing your mind and allowing me to go to appease me?" he asked. "I'm not trying to make you do anything you don't want to do. I'm hoping that between us, we can choose to do what's right for Gary and us. I know his relationship with his father is at stake. But it seems that our relationship is also getting challenged by this. I have to fight for it, and I hope you will too," he implored.

They sat quietly for a few minutes, staring at each other. Tears streamed down Maxi's face as she spoke up. "Tony, my life with you and Gary is my most treasured possession.

I don't want to mess it up, and I don't want anything (especially Devin and his demands) to mess it up. But how do we get past this issue and back to where we were?" she asked.

"Well, first off, I'm going with you. Not to posture or get in any confrontation. I will support you and show the strength of what Gary has with us—together. Then we both must acknowledge that maybe *we* aren't as perfect as we think. We have work to do. We have to move forward, but we have some work to do so we don't come back here again. Right now, though, we better go get ready, so we don't show up late," he replied.

"Okay," Maxi said, standing and clearing the table.

"I'll take care of that," Tony said, taking the dish from her hand and setting it in the sink before holding her tightly and rocking her back and forth.

"Thanks, babe, for everything," Maxi said, smiling as she looked up at Tony.

Tony kissed her loudly and said, "Go get dressed. I'll take care of cleaning the dishes and then come do the same. You know you're kind of slow changing outfits ten times and whatnot," he said.

"Whatever," Maxi replied as they both chuckled.

Gary was at the park with his friends, so Maxi left a note in case he returned home before they did. She didn't specifically say where they were going but indicated they would be back between two and three o'clock. Then Maxi and Tony strolled down the steps, holding hands, on their way to meet with Devin.

Maxi folded her finger between Tony's anxiously, squeezing tightly. *I pray Devin is on his best behavior, and I'll try to be on mine, especially so Tony doesn't think he has to defend me.*

Tony could feel the stress emanating from Maxi, so he stopped, put his arms around her shoulder, then turned her toward him, hugged her, and held her chin as he asked, "Nervous?"

"A little. I don't want a scene," Maxi said, unable to ignore her thoughts.

"There will not be a scene, Max. Well, unless he wants one." Tony chuckled as he brushed her hair back from her face.

"See what I mean, Tony!" Maxi responded frantically.

"Okay, okay. That was a joke! Smile, laugh," Tony begged. "Max, I'm not going to start anything. I love Gary, too. I want to meet the guy. I'm sure he wants to meet the guy that's been taking care of his son as a father since he's been on hiatus. I want him to know I'm here for you and Gary. Okay?" Tony finished.

"Okay. Thanks, baby. Honestly. It's so good having you with me."

Tony kissed Maxi before wrapping his arms around her again and rocking from side to side. "I'm always going to be right by your side," he comforted her. "Now, I think we better get going to meet Gary's father. Ready?"

Maxi answered unconvincingly, "Yes, let's go."

"We'll play it by ear. I've got your back no matter what," Tony consoled Maxi.

Maxi nodded, and her smile said she was thankful for Tony's support and company.

They walked the remainder of the way quietly, holding hands. As they arrived at the eatery, Maxi sighed heavily.

Tony stroked her hair as a show of support. They entered and looked around. To their left, in the far corner, Maxi caught the glassy gray-blue stare.

"Oh, there he is," she said with a tone of relief and disappointment all rolled together.

They strolled to the booth. Devin stood up as he noticed them approaching. Tony stepped almost before Maxi, stretched his hand, and introduced himself.

"Hey, man. Tony. Nice to meet you."

Devin shook his hand. "Hey, Tony. Devin. My son talks about you a lot."

"Oh, yeah?" asked Tony.

"Yeah," replied Devin.

"He's a great kid," Tony responded.

"Yes, he is. He is," Devin said, nodding affirmatively.

Maxi stood there, arms folded, bewildered by this seeming lovefest. *What kind of tricks does Devin have up his sleeve? Is he trying to play us?*

"Hey, Maxine. Long time," Devin said, smiling slightly.

"Yes. It's definitely been a long time. Hi, Devin," Maxi countered with a professional tone.

"I guess we should sit, huh?" Devin continued.

Devin sat on one side of the booth, and Tony and Maxi sat on the other.

"Hey, Devin, I know you and Maxi need to talk about your son. I'm not here to intrude. I care about Gary, and, of course, this is my wife. I want to make sure they're good, and they get whatever they need. I wanted to meet you and say hello because I don't want to start with negative vibes between us."

Tony hesitated for a second, looked directly at Maxi,

and continued. "But I will leave and give you space to discuss what you all need. I'll be back for my wife," he said as he searched Maxi's face for a reaction.

Maxi smiled and said, "Thanks, babe. Maybe forty-five minutes or so, uh?" She looked over at Devin for confirmation.

"I ain't got no problem with that," Devin answered.

"All right then. I'll be back in a little while," Tony replied.

Tony kissed Maxi and commented, "I'll be up at the bowling alley. I need some practice to beat that twelve-year-old upstart."

Maxi returned the kiss, nodded, and responded with a smile, "Yeah, get that work in."

Tony shook Devin's hand again and exited the eatery.

"He seems like an all-right guy. Gary only had good things to say about him, as I said before. He's got a little baby face there, though, Maxine. What is he? Like eight or ten years younger than you? But that ain't my worry, huh?" questioned Devin.

Maxi stared coldly at Devin but didn't respond.

"Maxine's eyes are saying, 'I'm not interested in small talk,'" Devin said, chuckling.

"You're right. We're wasting precious time out of the forty-five-minute time limit we set, and I'm here about Gary, not Tony," Maxi replied coolly.

Devin placed both elbows on the table and clasped his fingers to support his chin as he stared at Maxi. "Hey, Maxine Desiree. How are you?"

"I'm fine, Devin," she answered.

Devin nodded. "Yep. Yep. That you are. You look good.

Actually, you look great."

Maxi did not respond.

"Aren't you even going to ask how I'm doing?" Devin asked, almost begging.

"Devin. I hope you are doing well. But we're here for a purpose. We are here to talk about Gary and your role in his life," she replied icily.

"Hmm. You're still all about business, aren't you, Maxine? I guess I deserve that," Devin answered, shaking his head.

By now, Maxi was frustrated. "Devin, maybe this wasn't such a good idea, and I should just go up to the bowling alley where my husband is," Maxi said while moving toward the end of the booth.

Devin reached over and covered her left hand with his right. "Don't, Maxine. I'm sorry. I'm sorry. Everything was going right for you back then, you know. And nothing was going right for me. It felt like you expected me to figure it out and figure it out quickly, and I couldn't. So, I hurt you. I knew your history with your father, and I knew what would hurt you, and I hurt you. The thing is, I didn't factor into the equation the pain to my son and even to me."

"Oh," replied Maxi, unsure what to say but searching Devin's eyes for more.

"Yeah, I know you're confused. Change is hard, Maxine. Actually, recognizing that you even need to make a change is hard. It took losing Cliff. It was sudden, and it was like losing my sight!" Devin revealed.

"Wait! Cliff, your cousin Cliff? What do you mean losing him?" Maxi asked, confused.

"He's gone, Maxine. Cliff passed away. It's been more

than a year now," Devin answered after taking a deep breath.

Cliff and Devin were the same age. Although they were cousins, they grew up together like brothers and always treated each other as such. But Devin was the leader and the popular one. Cliff was the one hanging on, needing to be in Devin's circle, trying to be like Devin but unable to command the attention and power. For most of their lives, they were rarely ever apart. But when Devin moved to Florida, he didn't just walk away from Maxi and Gary; he walked away from Cliff too. Caught up in his own troubles and concerns, Devin ignored what everyone else knew: Cliff was lost without him. In January 1996, D.C. had one of its biggest snowstorms. Family members were concerned after not hearing from Cliff for several days. No one answered his phone, and a visit turned up an empty apartment with his wallet and coat sitting on the sofa. Days later, the police found his body, barefooted and dressed only in pajamas. Of course, he had died of hypothermia. Why he was out in the snow and cold, dressed as he was, is still a mystery. But his family surmised that his action was the result of depression.

"I didn't know. Nobody told me," Maxi said after hearing the story. *I know Devin shut us off, but I must admit that I shut his family off too.*

"Well, it was probably on the news. I don't really know," Devin said after taking another deep breath. "I just know I didn't deal with that well for a while, either. I didn't come home for the funeral. I felt like I was in a daze for months. Anxiety got the best of me for a while. Then, one day, I was walking into my apartment, and this kid came out bouncing a basketball and said, "Hey, Mister, I just moved in here. Do you have a son that can play with me?" Devin continued saying the words as though he were in a trance. "He looked like Gary, and I had a flashback to playing with Gary, and I figured nowadays he would be about that kid's size. It made me wonder what Gary was doing and what he needed. I remembered that we never got a chance to hold our first baby Maxine. I will never forget that. But we have Gary, he's here, and I know how happy we were when he was born. You see Maxine, that incident with the kid made me wonder if my son was alone and did, he need someone to play with. Did he need me, and I wasn't there? I realized I had let him down and I wanted to change that," he continued.

Maxi was speechless. She sat frozen.

"I had to tell you that before we even talked about Gary because I thought you ought to know my motive. I want a relationship with my son. I know you have moved on. I will respect that, especially given how your husband approached me to introduce himself but still gave us space and time to talk. But don't worry. I'm not coming after you. I only want a chance with my son, Maxine," Devin continued, seeming genuine.

Maxi rifled through her purse, pulled out a tissue, and dabbed her tears.

"I appreciate your apology," she said. "I know it wasn't easy. And, if back then, I didn't recognize that you were looking to me for some direction, *I* apologize. I was busy building my foundation so I wouldn't depend on you or anybody else. I was young. You were young. What's done is done. But Gary is here. He wants us both, and he needs us both. I'll do my part if you do your part," Maxi offered in return.

"I'm ready, Maxine. I'm ready to be a father to my son. I've talked to him almost every day for the past two to three months, trying to catch up on six years. Maybe that's where *we* should start. You can share milestones and memories from the past six years with me. Then day by day, I can pick up with him," Devin suggested.

Devin got the waiter's attention and ordered drinks and appetizers. Maxi pulled out her wallet and displayed an array of pictures, sharing the year, the moment, and its significance with Devin. She answered his questions and did her best to fill in the information he was missing about the years he had been away. They were still engrossed in catching up when Tony returned.

"Need some more time?" he asked, slowly approaching the table.

"Hey, baby. Oh, wow, forty-five minutes flew by. Come sit down," Maxi said, shifting to the booth's corner. They closed the conversation with Maxi agreeing that Devin could pick up Gary from school each day (and even take him), but he would consult with her about other visits or outings. This meeting was their starting point. What else would come out of it was unknown. But this was their new beginning.

Before thanking them, both and leaving the eatery, Devin handed Maxi a card in a sealed envelope. Peering at Tony to put him at ease, he said, "Just something to hold onto for Gary."

"Thanks," Maxi said, puzzled.

After Devin left, Maxi laid her head on Tony's shoulder and let out a big sigh.

"That bad?"

"Oh no, not at all. I'm just relieved that it wasn't that bad. You never know from day to day, but I'm not afraid we'll be playing tug-of-war with Gary. Right now, I'm feeling positive."

"What's in the envelope?"

"Nosy," Maxi said, giggling. "I don't know, but let's see."

There was a note card in Devin's handwriting.

> *Maxine Desiree,*
>
> *Thank you for caring for our son and filling his life with love. Thank you for being kind because you had every chance to come after me and take everything I had, and you didn't. I can never repay you or Gary but know I never lost sight of my responsibility. I am ready to be in his life as a father and am prepared to share my heart and fulfill my obligations emotionally and financially, starting with this.*
>
> *Sincerely,*
>
> *Devin*

The note was attached to the documentation for savings bonds. Devin had purchased savings bonds for Gary since Gary was a baby and had continued over the years that he was gone. Maxi was astounded. *A nest egg for college or even starting a business. It was up to Gary to decide, but knowing he had this foundation opened up his options.*

Maxi shared the documents with Tony. "It's a start, huh? I don't know if, after today, the 'Devin storm' will be over, but I know I can handle it if it comes around again."

"That's the 'Maxi spirit' that I know and love," Tony said, hugging her. Maxi returned his hug with a smile. She breathed a sigh of relief because the meeting with Devin

had gone so much better than expected. Then she remembered that Nancy's response to her counteroffer was still
pending. *Ugh, one down and one to go!*

CHAPTER

# EIGHT

All in all, it was a great weekend. Maxi was happy that Gary didn't need to sneak around anymore to spend time with his father, and she was relatively comfortable with how she and Tony would interact with Devin. Also, Maxi and Tony were proactively taking time to discuss their concerns and insecurities. And they even included a Sunday movie date night. For Maxi, this situation had been an eye-opener on how much she still sought to control every life event in hopes of protecting herself. It wasn't going to be easy, but she knew she had to be more willing to let go of the reins and, most of all, careful never to shut her husband out, especially when it was a family-impacting event or situation.

But now it was Monday morning. It was time to head

back to work and get the company's response to her proposal for taking on more responsibility and getting compensated despite the layoffs.

When Maxi arrived at the office, she took a deep breath before entering the lobby. *Another day in the glass towers. I pray there won't be any stone-throwing today. I need to continue working on the reports for my portfolio and tackle those in Melissa's. Let's see what else is on tap.* Maxi powered on her computer and opened her email. *For crying out loud! DEFAULT. Default, what in the world? Here it is again. How does another account, with over five million dollars on hand, default on a two hundred-thousand-dollar payment? I should look at the recent transactions and reports first, but I won't. It must be that silly error again. I don't get why we have a recurrence. These defaults can't become a regular thing. What time is it? Seven forty-five. I'll reach out at eight o'clock. And this time, I'm not being nice. It's ridiculous.*

Maxi went to the break room to grab a cup of tea to start the day. It was a little early, so Maxi was surprised to see Victoria from the receivables and payables staff there.

"Morning, Victoria. Have a good weekend?" Maxi asked cordially.

"Morning, Maxi. It was good. And now, here I am, back to the grind," Victoria answered, grinning.

"I hear you. But we've gotta do what we've gotta do, right?" Maxi replied in agreement.

"Yes, we do. Bills to pay that won't just magically go away," Victoria quipped.

"That's for sure," said Maxi.

"Well, you have a good day," Maxi said.

"You too," Victoria responded.

Maxi turned to exit the break room, tea mug in hand, when Victoria called out, "Oh, Max, I need to come by and see you today."

"Me?" Maxi asked, surprised.

"Yes, yes. I had a question about some payments for a client in Melissa's portfolio, and, well, since she isn't here, I think maybe you're it," she said, shrugging her shoulders.

"Well, I don't know about me being *it!* But if I can help answer a question or point you in the right direction, I'm willing to do so," Maxi replied.

"Thanks, Max, that would be great," Victoria said with a sigh of relief.

*Max? When did our relationship reach the level where she could call me "Max"? We've always been professional and courteous. However, I have never had a conversation with this woman that went deeper than the weather or general banter about the weekend. Maybe I'm making a big deal out of nothing, but she doesn't have permission to "Max" me. See, now I'm getting worked up about the bank and Victoria. What's next? Ouch, here I am again, getting ahead of myself, thinking I know people's motives, and trying to always be in control. Let me breathe and let it go.*

After giving her bank contact a good scolding, Maxi emailed a reprimand with an indirect warning regarding the renewal of the firm's contract with the bank. Having put out that fire, she focused on further developing the mid-year reports. She made good headway until Victoria poked her head in the door's opening.

"Hey there, do you have a minute now?" Victoria called out to Maxi.

*Well, at least she didn't say "Max."* Maxi looked up from

her computer, smiled, and beckoned to Victoria, "Sure, come on in."

Victoria entered, carrying several folders. "Thank you. I know I popped in without notice, but it shouldn't be too long. You see, these invoices came in, and typically Melissa signs off on them, but Nancy told me on Friday that from now on, you should sign off on them," replied Victoria.

*Wow. That's interesting. I thought this was all still up for discussion. I haven't heard from Nancy today, although she said she would get back to me by Monday. But I guess the day isn't over, so I'll play along.*

"Well, I think she meant that for the short term, you know since I do similar work and have the experience," Maxi replied. "Is that the client folder you have?" she continued.

"Yes, yes. We could go through it together, and you could direct me," Victoria answered.

"A question first—when are those payments due? I doubt they are due today, right?" Maxi asked.

"No, these are due at the end of the week. But, since I figured it would be something additional on your plate, I wanted to get ahead of the game and have you look at the documents and approve them now," Victoria answered.

"Hmm. Here's what I'll do. You leave that folder and the bills with me, and I will review them and get back to you with directions. I heard your deadline, and I'll make sure you get an answer on time," Maxi said, smiling courteously.

"Oh, you can't just sign off now?" Victoria asked.

"No, that would not be the way to do it. But I know what's needed, so leave it, and I'll respond," Maxi replied with a piercing stare and a frozen smile.

"Okay," Victoria said, slowly standing, pushing the folder forward on Maxi's desk, and exiting the office.

*Who does she think I am? I'm not stupid. Like I'm going to sign off on something she shoves in my face. No! Now I know that if this deal goes down, I must watch that one closely. These people's money isn't something to play with, and I'm not getting myself fired over foolishness. Goodness. I'll look at the folder later and confer with Nancy. I don't know who's been talking to Victoria about my responsibilities, but they ought to find the time to speak to me.*

It was close to the end of the day, and Maxi still hadn't heard from Nancy. Maxi was reviewing the contents of the folder Victoria had left with her when she was suddenly interrupted.

"Hey."

Maxi looked up to see Nancy standing at her office door. "Hey," Maxi responded.

"Well, here's the deal. I discussed your request with my boss. He will go with your requirements if you guarantee that you're not going anywhere for the rest of this year," Nancy shared.

"Going anywhere? What are you saying?" Maxi asked. She understood what Nancy was asking but was taken aback by this mandate, so she acted as though she had no clue.

Nancy pushed the office door to close it. "Maxi, if they do something special for you, then come on, they want a commitment."

"Nancy, so you want me to commit? Are you giving me a commitment that you will not lay me off next month or the month after that or the month after that or let me go some-time in the next two years?" Maxi asked with attitude.

"Maxi, I can't tell you what to do, but don't make this too hard, okay?" Nancy said.

"I'm not making it hard," said Maxi. "And while I can tell you that I'm not actively looking, I will never give anyone a written guarantee that I won't go if someone proactively seeks me out and offers me a better deal than this. Seri-ously, Nancy, you guys aren't even giving me a raise to do this, and you want me to sign an oath?" she continued, up-set.

"No one is asking you to sign an oath, Maxi." Nancy stared at Maxi. "Look, I'll go back and try to talk him through this to bypass any guarantees or oaths. You've never given me a reason not to trust you, and so I'm going to believe you won't suddenly pack up and leave," she said, searching Maxi's face for acknowledgment.

Maxi's stoic stare didn't reveal much. Nancy stood up. "I'll get back to you," she said, exiting Maxi's office.

*The nerve! They want to hold me hostage, for a pittance, and Nancy is posturing as though I ought to be grateful. It's a two-way street; they ought to be grateful to have me! And I don't know what the deal is, but the hits keep coming. When-ever I think the storm is over, I feel the wind stirring and raindrops hitting me.*

Maxi returned to the file Victoria had left with her, try-ing to ensure that she covered all the bases before signing off when again Nancy poked her head inside the office door. "It's a go!" Nancy declared, raising her thumb.

"Great. That was quick! But thank you. I appreciate you going to bat for me," Maxi replied with gratitude.

"Of course, Maxi. You're like my right hand. I don't want to lose you," Nancy said sincerely.

"Ah, Nancy. We make a great team. We'll get this done," Maxi responded calmly.

"Good. I'm going to head out for the day. We'll meet tomorrow and bring in Sally and Victoria once we hash out our training plan and responsibilities. I did send Victoria your way on one thing. But over the coming weeks we'll formalize the supervisory aspects of the work team," Nancy continued.

"That works. I'll be out the door shortly as well," Maxi answered.

"Have a good evening, Maxi," Nancy said.

"You do the same, Nancy," Maxi replied.

As soon as Nancy left her office, Maxi turned her back to the door and unleashed a big smile. *See, my instincts were right! They weren't ready to start from scratch with no knowledge base in this area and no true leader to back up Nancy. But they will try to get away with whatever they can. The best-case scenario for them would have been tricking me into accepting their "bone" of a team lead designation without any compensation. I'm so glad I didn't take the safe route and cave. My quarterly bonuses will be a win for our home renovation fund. Then I will get that official title by the end of the year, and if things improve with the company, I will ask for a position title change and salary upgrade before the end of the year!*

Maxi grabbed the phone and dialed; she had to tell Tony now. She repeated her two exchanges with Nancy nearly word for word, with Tony cheering her on the whole time. He was beaming with pride, and she was overjoyed at her achievement.

"My baby is doing big things. I'm always proud of you, Max. But for this one I'm going to bring home something special for you!" he declared.

"Tony, no. No funny stuff. I know you," she replied.

"Oh, come on, Max. You don't trust me?" he said, laughing out loud.

"I trust you, but I know who you are, so don't bring anything home. I know it's Monday, but we'll go out for a change. We'll go early so Gary won't be out too late," she said.

"Well, where are we going? The bowling alley?" Tony asked, bellowing uncontrollably. "I do need to get some more practice in."

Sweetly smiling, Maxi answered, "Tony Vernay, I love you, but no bowling alley today. Anyway, let me get out of here to get home at a decent hour. Plus, they're calling for a thunderstorm; maybe I can beat it home. But I'm so happy that if the sky opened up and showers poured down, you won't see me running for cover; instead, you'll find me dancing in the rain!"

Writings by Jackie

# ABOUT
# THE AUTHOR

A motivational blogger and self-published author, Jacqueline P. Walker (Jackie), writes to inspire, entertain, and connect with readers to share and gain insight while building bridges across cultures.

She previously self-published a memoir of perseverance and overcoming obstacles, "A Season of Disruption." Jackie has also contributed motivational articles for the Everyday Power inspirational website/blog. And, her personal essay, "Disrupted Not Defeated," appears in The Caribbean Writer - Volume 36 (an international, refereed literary journal with a Caribbean focus published annually by the University of the Virgin Islands).

# Dancing in the Rain

*A Novella*

https://amazon.com/author/writingsbyjackie

www.writingsbyjackie.com

https://sociatap.com/JWalkerPat